The Circle Dance

Jen Silver

The Circle Dance

Jen Silver

Affinity
eBook Press
NZ

2016

The Circle Dance

© Jen Silver 2016

Affinity E-Book Press NZ LTD
Canterbury, New Zealand

1st Edition

ISBN: 978-0-908351-69-5

All rights reserved.

Editor: Angela Koenig
Proof Editor: Alexis Smith
Cover Design: Irish Dragon Designs

Acknowledgments

Heartfelt thanks, as always, to the Affinity team. They continually show remarkable patience and understanding in dealing with an anxious author from the other side of the world.

I would like to acknowledge the work of beta editors Mel and Mary—not an easy task when faced with alien terminology from the British Isles. The ever vigilant Angela undertook the final edit stage.

This story wasn't easy to write on many levels but mostly I'm grateful to the cyclists stopping in the town on their long distance Sunday rides who were willing to answer my questions.

Thank you also to my long-suffering partner, Anne, who thought my retirement from work meant we would be spending more time together. Instead she's putting up with me going into writing mode for several hours a day and then disappearing off to conferences or archaeology digs.

Perhaps to the disappointment of family members who no doubt figured they were next in line for a dedication, this book is dedicated to a cat who touched the lives of many through his Facebook page. Spencer P. Moran was the inspiration for the feline character who plays a significant role in this story. I am grateful, therefore, to the late Sandra Moran for giving permission for one of Spencer's poems to be printed with the Dedication. As a highly talented writer and all round wonderful human being, Sandra is also greatly missed by everyone who had the good fortune to know her through her work and humorous interactions via Facebook.

Dedication

For Spencer P. Moran, a cat of many talents, who was much loved and is sadly missed.

I see you,
birds,
of a feather,
flocking,
together ...
in fellowship.
It warms my heart
to see you
clustered together.
A clutch.
A flock.
A gaggle.
And, it makes it
Easier.
for me
to hunt you.

May you rest in peace, Spencer...your life, as expressed in your poetry, enriched the lives of your many devoted Facebook friends. Happy hunting!

Also by Jen Silver

The Starling Hill Trilogy
Starting Over
Arc Over Time
Carved in Stone

There Was a Time (Short Story)
The Christmas Sweepstake (Affinity's 2014 Christmas
Collection)

Table of Contents

Chapter One

Sasha Fairfield looked at the pile of manuscripts with dismay. They represented not just a lot of unread, and in some cases, unreadable words, but also a host of anxious writers wondering why they hadn't heard yet whether their work of art was likely to ever be seen by a publisher. The life of a literary agent wasn't all Harry Potter and Fifty Shades. But she had to keep an open mind for there might be a gem hidden in this lot.

Stevie jumped up onto her lap and gave her his green-eyed stare, which always made her think of Jamie. Her ex-lover's eyes were brown but it was the same intense look. She stroked Stevie and he settled down on her lap and, not for the first time in the last few months, she wished she could be stroking Jamie. It was a mystery to her now why she had thrown away the best relationship she'd ever had. For what? To satisfy an urge? An illusion? A distraction at best? She had found the first few months with her new lover exciting in and out of bed. They shared a passion for fiction and

Phoebe's enthusiasm for discussing books was endless, whereas Jamie's idea of good reading material started and ended with computer manuals.

"Do you miss her, too?" she whispered. The black cat opened one eye briefly and continued purring. She thought he did, he just wasn't going to admit it.

It was Jamie who had named Stevie. Thinking he was female when they brought him home from the cat rescue shelter, she had named him after her favourite singer, Stevie Nicks. Good thing it hadn't been Adele. His gender had been revealed when they took him to the vet for routine shots and were told he was male. By that time they had decided the name Stevie suited him.

Sasha found herself dwelling more and more on her life with Jamie. It had been good, more than good. She had loved the way Jamie looked after her, opened doors, always put her first. In return she had held Jamie's heart. But somewhere along the way she'd dropped it. Surely she wasn't so shallow as to have been affected by listening to the way her friends put Jamie down at every opportunity. "For God's sake, Sash. It doesn't matter how good she is in bed, eventually you need someone with a brain."

Jamie had every reason to hate her for the way she'd behaved. She had turned into the bitch from hell and she hadn't even registered the hurt in Jamie's eyes the last time she'd seen her.

And now Jamie had disappeared. The solicitor dealing with the house sale hadn't been able to tell Sasha where she had moved, deflecting her enquiry with some sort of client confidentiality bullshit. Always a fan of social media, Jamie had withdrawn from that as well. No sign of her on Facebook or Twitter. But as a highly qualified computer whiz she could have set up other accounts in another name. There was only one option left. Trying to find her at her place of work, the location of which Sasha had carefully extracted from a mutual friend. It felt like stalking. But the need to connect with Jamie was getting stronger and harder to ignore.

Sasha sighed and picked up the first page of the novel on top of the pile. *The Moons of Septimus Seven* by Felix LeMar. Did this author really think they could write like Philip K Dick? Why send it to her? Smoke Rising Publishing didn't deal in fantasy or sci-fi.

Well, this shit wasn't going to read itself, unfortunately. She'd try the first twenty pages and then it was toast.

†

The doctor looked down at her patient and sighed. "Do you think you could relax a bit more?"

"You know I hate this. I'm only having it done because you say I have to."

"It just takes a few seconds. Lie back and think of something pleasant."

"Like what? When I know you're going to plunge that cold metal thing into me…"

"Don't be such a baby…and it's plastic."

Jamie Steele closed her eyes and gripped the sides of the bench firmly. "Do your worst, Doc." She braced her feet as well and prepared for the moment of agony.

It was over quickly, as the doctor had said, although Jamie did let out a squeak when the speculum was pulled out.

"All done. Get dressed and come through to my office."

Jamie had chosen her garments carefully for the occasion and quickly pulled on her soft cotton briefs and sweats. She went into the doctor's office and sat gingerly on the edge of the chair.

"I don't care what you say, it still hurts. How many more of these tests do I have to endure?"

"Let me see. You'll be fifty in December, so only two, possibly three more after this. Every five years. Although I see you managed to stretch this examination to six."

"Well, I had reminders coming through my door as frequently as letters from Hogwarts for a certain boy wizard. I couldn't ignore them any longer. The arrival of owls might have upset the neighbours."

"It didn't have anything to do with the fact that you're coming round for dinner tonight and wouldn't be able to escape."

"Don't tell me you have these instruments of torture at home? I don't know how Laurel puts up with you." Jamie imitated the doctor's voice. "Oh, don't put the veg on yet, dear. I'm just going to give our guest a smear test."

"Very funny." Dr Madeleine Hope leant back in her chair and gave her friend a stern look over the top of her glasses. "Seriously though, you don't look like you're eating properly. You've lost weight since I last saw you."

Jamie stared at her feet. The problem with having a doctor as a friend, nothing got past her. She hadn't been eating properly for some time. Ever since the abrupt departure of her girlfriend of six years, the one she thought she would be spending the rest of her life with. Sasha's timing had been shit as well. Jamie had just found out the promotion she had hoped for was going to someone else and she was being made redundant. Arriving home that day to share the bad news with her partner, a shoulder to cry on, she was greeted instead by a note on the kitchen table and empty spaces in the closet.

She picked at a loose thread on her sweat pants, unable to meet the sympathy she knew would be in her friend's eyes. Standing abruptly, she said, "See you later," and made it out to the street before the tears started to leak out. Jamie walked quickly up the hill and then ran up the steep steps leading to her rented room. There was no time to give in to the pain of the past. The early morning appointment with the doctor meant she was on a tight schedule to get changed and head off to work.

Cycling up the long incline towards Halifax, Jamie thought about meeting Maddie during her first week at university. It didn't seem likely she would be friends with a medical student, figuring she had to come from a posh background. Jamie was making ends meet with a part time job in a bicycle shop. Piecework—getting paid for each bike she assembled—skills gained in childhood when her dad first showed her how to repair an inner tube and maintain her ancient three-speed Raleigh.

Maddie, it turned out, was doing shifts in a bar, determined to contribute to her tuition fees and repay the faith her mother had shown in working three jobs to make sure she could fulfil her dream of becoming a doctor.

As the university buildings came into view, Jamie switched her thoughts from the past, to concentrate on weaving through the final set of lights to make it to the campus in one piece.

†

Handled that well, doc, Maddie berated herself. *Note: must work on bedside manner.*

She finished filling in the form to send Jamie's smear test off to the lab and closed down her notes on the computer. Having managed to fit Jamie in before the regular start of surgery hours, she had a few minutes before her next patient arrived.

It had been a shock to see how much Jamie had changed when they met up again at the university alumni reunion the previous year. Gone was the cocky, slightly pudgy teenager she remembered from their early acquaintance at the Gaysoc social for freshers. They had hung out together for a while during the first year before the demands of her coursework drove them apart. The rigours of studying medicine didn't leave much room for a social life. At the reunion, it was Jamie who had recognised her straight away and spoken to her. It took Maddie a few moments to realise who she was. The baby fat had disappeared and it looked like she worked out. But it was the lines around the eyes and an edginess in her demeanour that really made the difference from the young woman she had known back then.

So much had happened in that thirty-year gap. She was married with two children, one of whom was about to set off to university himself. And Jamie, it seemed, was suffering from a recent disintegration of a long-term relationship. When they talked at the reunion, Maddie had been enthusing about Hebden Bridge and how much they enjoyed living there. And Jamie had seized on that, asking her for details. She was ready for a change of scene. The house she and her partner had owned jointly in Bury was taking a long time to sell. But she couldn't wait to move away from the memories. So, Maddie had encouraged her to take a look at the town. If she could find somewhere cheap to rent, it could be just the lift needed to make the break and start building a new life.

Maddie pulled out her mobile and called home. Laurel answered right away. "What's up, hon?"

Even after twenty years together, Laurel's voice warmed her.

"I've just seen Jamie. You were right; I don't think she's coping very well. I'm not sure about the plans for this evening."

"Don't worry. Van's been briefed."

"I just don't think she's ready to move on yet."

"It's been a year. She just needs to get out more."

A timid knock on the door reminded Maddie that her next patient was waiting. "Okay, but please tell Van to take it easy. She can be a bit full on at times." The doctor ended the call, put the phone down on her desk, and called out, "Come in."

†

Van Spencer stared at her computer screen. It stared blankly back. Only an hour to go and she would be out of here. No more listening to the woman in the next cubicle talking loudly on the phone to a friend. They were talking about a TV programme. Not anything Van had seen but she could have recited the plot backwards by now. She wouldn't be suffering through the vivid descriptions of who did what to whom if their supervisor hadn't disappeared for a managerial meeting. Mobiles were supposed to be left in their lockers during working hours.

She thought about the dinner that evening. Deciding what to wear hadn't been difficult even though she suspected Laurel was trying to set her up with someone. Okay, so she'd been out of the dating scene for a while. That wasn't unexpected given the disastrous nature of her last affair. She would definitely be reading the small print before clicking the "Agree" button anytime soon. So Laurel's text to remind her to take it slowly with their other guest was hardly necessary. She wasn't planning to jump the woman's bones as soon as they were introduced.

All she knew was that this Jamie person was more a friend of the doc's than of Laurel. They had been at university together and only got back in touch when Jamie showed up at an alumni reunion, evidently still suffering from a painful breakup. Did she really need to hook up with someone with that sort of baggage? Still, at her age, it was unlikely she was going to find anyone travelling light, unless she wanted to try cradle snatching. And that really wasn't an option.

Only two weeks ago she had celebrated her forty-fifth birthday—if you could call it a celebration—with her parents. Her mother tactlessly mentioned Haley, and only realised her faux pas when her father, Van was sure, had kicked her under the table. Van turned it into the now well-worn family joke, that like the comet of the same name, her ex should only be mentioned once every seventy-five years.

"Hey, Van. You joining us for a drink after work?" The question came from the cubicle to her left. Looking up she saw Connor leering at her, head resting on the top of the divider.

"Nope. Got a date."

"You're kidding."

"Why would I be kidding? You think I'm too old to have a date?" Connor was twenty and no doubt thought Van was old enough to be his gran, tucked up in bed with a mug of cocoa by eight o'clock on a Friday night.

"Well, no, but…"

"Well, yes, but. You do." She enjoyed teasing him. "So, any chat up lines you can suggest, stud?"

He turned red and his ears looked more prominent than usual.

Loopy Lou, as she thought of her, had finished her phone conversation and decided to join in. "Who's the lucky woman, Van?"

"No one you know." Van's screen lit up with an incoming chat request. She looked at the clock; time to give the customer the benefit of her wisdom. "Sorry, guys. I'll have to take this one."

As she typed out instructions for "distressed of Denton" who couldn't figure out how to change their pin number, she mentally ran through her exit plan. She had her overnight bag with her. A quick stop at M&S for a bottle of wine, then leg it to the station—just time to catch the next train stopping at Hebden Bridge. And time to have a shower and change when she reached Laurel's house. And maybe time to thrash Leo on one of his Xbox games. At eighteen years old and preparing to start his first year at university studying physics, he thought he was good, but there were still a few things she could teach him. The thought made her smile, forgetting she was being set up for a blind date.

†

Carrying the bike up to her room on the top floor was hard work but she was fitter than she had ever been. The last six months had been tough but the move had helped. Jamie put the bicycle down to get out her key. The door opened into a large attic space. She had been pleased to find it knowing she wouldn't get anything else so close to the town centre with such a low rent. The lack of kitchen facilities was no hardship with an abundance of cafés and restaurants nearby, including a handy Thai takeaway.

Placing the bike against the wall, she went over to the window. It was a great view, looking out over the valley and the tops of the trees. She put her iPod in the docking station and restarted the album she'd been listening to on the ride home from work. Sasha had cleared out their CD collection so she'd had to download her favourites onto the small device. All on the Cloud now. No one could take them away from her again.

With Annie Lennox's voice giving vent to "A Whiter Shade of Pale," she stripped off her riding gear and got into the small shower stall. The water took a few minutes to warm up but the initial coolness gave her some relief from the heat generated by her ride. Washing between her legs she was relieved to find that the sting had gone. Peeing had been uncomfortable for most of the day after her early morning visit to the doctor. Maddie was right. She had put off having the regulation smear test for as long as possible. Her last experience with a male doctor had been excruciatingly painful—the bastard hadn't even bothered to warm his hands—and she'd sworn she would never have another cervical smear test, ever. When the letters kept coming from the local surgery, she had finally talked to her friend and said she would only go through with the procedure if Maddie did it. Well, it was done now. She could forget about the whole ghastly experience for the next five years at least.

Putting on a clean pair of black jeans along with a magenta and white striped Oxford shirt, she studied herself in the small mirror by the door. With her short brown hair brushed back, did she look too butch? Was there such a thing as looking too butch? And did it really matter? Whoever it was Laurel was trying to set her up with, they would have to take her or leave her. And the way she felt at the moment, being left was fine with her.

She tucked her reading glasses into her top pocket and checked she had her key and a tenner in her pocket, just in case. There wasn't likely to be a just in case since she was walking to her friends' house. But, on the other hand, if she found she couldn't face a few hours enduring sympathetic smiles and conversational glitches, she could always head off to the pub and find a quiet corner where she could play *Super Stickman Golf* on her phone. She had never played actual golf but the virtual game was fun.

Out in the open she started to feel better as she walked through the park onto the canal towpath. September was one of her favourite months as a crispness started to return to the air and the leaves began changing colour. Annie was now singing "Walking On Broken Glass" and Jamie switched the music off, stuffing the ear buds in her pocket before the words filled her head with more sadness.

She turned off the path and began the climb that led to the doctor's house near the top of the hill. With the hours commuting on the bike and the number of steps up to her room, she was able to make this journey without having to stop every few minutes to catch her breath. When she reached the driveway leading up to the house, she saw that Maddie's Freelander wasn't there which meant she would be alone with Laurel for a bit. Perhaps she would have time to find out something about the so-called date before they had to be introduced.

Laurel Chambers was a music teacher. She gave piano lessons at home and also did after-school sessions three days a week at the local high school. When Jamie met her for the first time at the reunion, Maddie introduced her as her wife and Jamie felt sorry for her old friend thinking the woman looked remote. She was stunningly attractive in a Nordic way—blonde hair piled up on her head, piercing blue eyes, a good few inches taller than her partner—an ice queen. Since getting to know the couple better over the last six months, Jamie realised this was mainly a front and had witnessed Laurel letting her hair down on a few occasions when she'd had more than one glass of wine.

The front door burst open just as she reached the flagged pathway. Jamie stopped to watch the youngster as she flew down the steps at breakneck speed.

"Hey, Tay. No need to break a leg to get your Mum's attention."

Taylor Hope stopped in mid-stride and launched herself at her. Jamie instinctively held onto the girl.

"What's up?" she asked gently, stroking the back of her head.

"Nothing," came the muffled response, hot lips brushing the side of her neck.

Jamie let go of the teenager and took a step back.

Tay grinned at her. "I just wanted to know what it feels like."

"Well, cut it out. Both your mums have drawers full of sharp knives and know how to use them." She studied the girl's outfit. Cut-off denim shorts that might have started out as thigh length now barely hugged her butt and were bordering on being called swimwear. Her sleeveless top was also showing more skin than should be legally allowed on a fully formed sixteen-year old. The chill in the almost-autumn air was making her nipples stand out. At least, Jamie hoped it was the cold and not the recent close contact with her body.

"Mm. Like what you see, James?"

"Taylor!" Laurel's voice reached them from the top of the steps. "You're not going out like that. Get back in here, now!"

"Aw, Mum." Tay turned to Jamie. "See what I have to put up with. She wants me to dress like a six-year old. It's Friday night, for Christ's sake."

"In! Now!"

Taylor started to trudge back up the steps.

"Hi, Jamie. Come on in." Laurel's voice softened as she addressed her. Jamie followed the girl, averting her eyes from the vision of long tanned legs disappearing into the frayed edges of the shorts.

†

Laurel took the casserole out of the oven. The vegetables were ready to be cooked but she would do them once everyone had arrived. Maddie was running late at the surgery as usual and Van had phoned to say her train was stuck at Littleborough.

She smiled at Jamie who was uncorking the red wine she'd brought. "So, when are you going to buy a place, J? You can't want to stay in that garret much longer."

"I like it."

"Yes, but now you've got the money from the house, you could find somewhere with more space, maybe even a garden."

"What do I need a garden for?" She yanked the cork out fiercely and looked around for the bin.

Laurel could have kicked herself. Of course, Sasha had done all the gardening in their old house. According to Jamie, not only had she come back shortly after she left to take most of their CD collection and a large number of DVDs, but she'd also carted off most of the plants from the garden.

"So, has Tay got a date?" Jamie asked as she poured wine for both of them.

Laurel led the way out to the conservatory. "I don't think so, but who knows what she gets up to once she leaves the house. We didn't have a moment's bother with Leo, but Taylor is testing us every way she can."

"She's just a different creature, more physical. You don't know what Leo might be up to online."

It was true, Laurel thought. Their daughter was very sporty and couldn't sit still for five minutes. Whereas Leo always had his head either in a math textbook or fixated on his computer screen.

"I don't think he's doing anything dodgy. Playing games on his Xbox against his friends is his main hobby."

"Ah, well. You never know. It's the quiet ones you have to watch out for."

Too true, thought Laurel, studying Jamie's profile. *And you're too quiet for your own good these days.*

They both sat watching a squirrel make its way carefully across the garden. The cat from next door was also watching closely from the top of the fence. The squirrel made it to safety and dashed up the nearest tree. The cat rearranged itself into a more comfortable position and closed its eyes.

"All right, Laurel. You might as well tell me. Who's this woman you want me to meet?"

"I think you'll like her. She does something with computers as well. Her name's Van."

"Short for Vanessa?"

"No. Her parents called her Ivana. They'd been reading Nabokov. She's always having to tell people she doesn't have any Russian roots."

"I guess she's lucky they didn't choose Lolita."

"Indeed!"

The doorbell chimed and Laurel leapt to her feet.

"That'll be her now. She's come straight from work so she'll want to use the shower and change. Maddie should be back soon. Help yourself to more wine."

Leaving Jamie to her thoughts, Laurel walked down the hall and opened the door to her friend.

"Sorry about that. Bloody trains. Hope dinner's not ruined."

"No. We haven't started yet. Maddie's still at the surgery."

"Okay. Good. I swear the climb up this hill gets longer. I'm sweating like a pig."

"Well, go hit the shower and join Jamie in the conservatory when you're presentable."

Laurel returned to the kitchen to check on her preparations. Time to make the salad dressing before Van came downstairs and Maddie arrived home.

†

The shower did its job, washing away the frustration of the last hour stuck on the train at Littleborough along with all the other Friday evening commuters who were wondering why they weren't moving out of the station. It was too early in September for the leaves-on-the-line excuse. There hadn't been any copious amounts of rain recently so the tunnel couldn't be flooded. No announcements were forthcoming. Everyone had their phones out either to call home or trawl the internet to see if there was any news of an incident on the track.

The passengers cheered loudly when the train finally moved and trundled at a slower pace than normal through the long tunnel to Walsden and beyond. Reaching Hebden Bridge an hour later than planned, Van hoped Laurel wasn't pissed off about delaying dinner. So it was a relief to find that Maddie wasn't home yet either.

Van dried her hair with the blow-dryer Laurel had thoughtfully left out for her and changed into her Friday night date clothes. They wouldn't be going out dancing, but she liked to look the part. Perhaps a sparkly, midnight-blue blouse wasn't appropriate for dinner with friends, but she had been told it brought out the colour of her eyes. The tight blue jeans were feeling a bit of a squeeze to get into these days. Maybe it was time she took up jogging again.

When she finally felt ready to meet the woman Laurel had said was just her type, she walked downstairs and out into the conservatory. Van was dismayed to see that young Taylor was already making a move on the woman perched on the edge of the two-seater.

"So, Jamie, do you think Mum will approve of this outfit?" Tay asked as she practically thrust her barely covered breasts into the startled Jamie's face.

"Tay! Give it a rest. Go out and play with your little friends."

Taylor turned and glared at Van, sticking her tongue out at her.

Van stuck her tongue out in response. Childish, she knew, but it had the desired effect. The girl got up and gave Jamie one last lingering glance before sashaying into the kitchen.

"Hi, I'm Van. Sorry about that. The brat's going through a Miley phase."

This comment at least drew a wry smile and Jamie stood to take her proffered hand. Nice, thought Van. In fact, much better than expected. Not just some loser pal of Maddie's who'd been dumped. With the elevated heels Van was wearing they were the same height and she found herself looking into deep brown eyes.

Whoa! Laurel really should have warned her. This one was cute, way too good looking to be let out on her own. The bitch who had broken her heart must be seriously demented.

"Jamie. Pleased to meet you."

Nice voice too. Not a local accent.

"Would you like a drink?"

Van smiled. An old fashioned butch. This evening was looking better and better. "Yes, please. A white wine, which I know Laurel has chilling in the fridge."

Jamie smiled back and Van thought she better sit down before she fell down. That was a killer smile.

"I'll be right back," Jamie said as she moved towards the kitchen.

Van watched her go. The back view wasn't bad either. What was her ex's problem? Did Jamie snore loudly, fart in public, or have chronic bad breath? Only one way to find out and Van wouldn't pass up the chance if it came along. Flirting wasn't something that came naturally to her, but tonight looked like a good time to practice.

Jamie returned, placing the glass of wine carefully on the table in front of her, within easy reach. "Laurel says you'll like this. It's the New Zealand one she usually buys."

It was no effort at all to give Jamie another warm smile. Van picked up the glass. "Cheers! Here's to the end of another working week!"

They clinked their glasses together and sipped in unison, taking each other's measure as they looked at each other over the rims.

Jamie put her glass down first and asked, quietly, "So, what do you do?"

It was as good a start as any. Van planned to keep her answers short as she wanted more than anything to hear more of Jamie's sexy voice.

†

"Hi honey, I'm home!" Maddie left her medical bag by the door and walked down the hall to the kitchen. The wonderful aroma assaulting her nostrils told her it was Laurel's famous *coq au vin* that was on the menu for this evening.

Her partner was stirring something at the stove, so she crept up behind and swept aside a lock of hair to kiss the back of her neck. "Something smells good," she whispered.

Laurel leant back into her and Maddie took the opportunity to wrap her arms around her waist. "Sorry I'm late. Do I have time to wash the blood off and get changed?"

It was an old joke but got a reaction each time. "Get your bloody hands off me, then."

Maddie pulled back and Laurel turned to face her.

"Are the others here?" the doctor asked.

"Yes, they're in the conservatory. So far, so good. However, you need to have words with your daughter."

"What's she done now?" Maddie sighed.

"She seems to think it's funny to come on to Jamie while wearing not much at all."

"Oh."

"Yes, oh. I've had to send her upstairs to change twice now." Laurel bent down and retrieved a covered plate from the oven. "Take this up to Leo. He's working on something and wants to stay in his room."

Lucky boy. Room service. "Okay. I won't be long."

Leo was engrossed in whatever was on his laptop, headphones on, tapping away. Maddie left the plate on his desk and moved down the hall to the next room. Her daughter was standing by the bed in her underwear contemplating an array of garments scattered across the duvet.

"Hey, trouble. What have you been up to now?"

"Nowt."

Maddie winced at the use of the colloquialism. But she knew better than to react. "Not what I've been told."

"Mum needs to chill."

"Yeah, right." Maddie walked over to the bed and looked at the clothing on display. "What is it this evening? A burlesque show?" She held up the strip of material that looked like it might be a skirt.

Taylor snatched it out of her hands. "No." She pouted, looking about ten. "Just meeting a few mates."

"Okay. So I expect you to be leaving the house wearing jeans and a sweatshirt."

"That's so boring."

"That's the deal. Or you'll be spending the evening here in your room. And I don't think that's what you want, unlike Leo."

"Oh, yeah. Mister Perfect." The lower lip was starting to tremble.

"Shit. Come here," Maddie hugged the girl and held her close. "We love you, sweetheart. Just the way you are."

After placating her daughter further by promising to take her snowboarding at the indoor ski slope the next day, Maddie left her to get dressed. Her own shower and change of clothes was completed in record time. She flicked her fingers through her shoulder length brown hair, deciding to let it dry naturally, and headed downstairs to see how their guests were getting on.

✝

Jamie had to admit it was the best meal she'd eaten in a while. She suspected Laurel was trying to fatten her up and twice turned down the offer of more potatoes. The conversation was flowing easily. Although she'd been wary about meeting this friend of Laurel's, the evening was turning out better than she'd thought it would.

Van Spencer wasn't what she'd expected either. She was funny and irreverent and Jamie had immediately felt at ease with her. They bonded, laughing about the foibles of their respective customers. If it wasn't for the fact that she was not looking for a relationship, she had to give Laurel credit for introducing her to someone who pushed all the right buttons. Van was attractive without being intimidating. Jamie could imagine running her fingers through the unruly mop of curly brown hair as she pulled the woman closer to kiss her full lips while two generous handfuls of breasts pressed against her, waiting to be explored.

Jamie took a deep breath. Maybe there was hope for her yet. She took a sip of wine and continued with the story she'd started about one of the more ludicrous help requests she'd dealt with recently.

"I got a call to go to a lecture room to see if I could get the equipment working. It was in Interactive Media session, and I thought, oh yeah, another knob-head professor who doesn't know how to unfreeze the whiteboard screen. I couldn't believe it, the twerp was using an overhead projector, which must have come out of a long-forgotten storage room and the light bulb had blown. The students were immensely relieved when I told him we didn't have a replacement. Death by PowerPoint is one thing, but death by OHP is infinitely worse."

They all laughed and Jamie caught Laurel smiling at Van. So it seemed their little conspiracy was working. Okay, she was happy to go along with it for now. She was enjoying herself and hadn't talked so much for a long time.

Laurel was definitely making an effort to draw her out and asked about her volunteering for the local Search and Rescue team. So Jamie explained that she had wanted to do something that got her out and about at weekends. She had done an orienteering course once upon a time and thought it would be a good way to get to know the area. Her probation period was almost over and the team was pleased with her fitness level, and her enthusiasm for trekking over the moors in wet and windy weather.

Sometime during the meal, Taylor came in wearing a pair of skinny jeans and a loose maroon sweatshirt. Maddie told her to come over and give her a kiss. Taylor complied, but Jamie noticed that Maddie was checking to see what was under the sweatshirt. She gave her daughter ten pounds and told her to be in by eleven. That drew a pout but the girl nodded and left.

"Why is that she listens to you and not me?" Laurel asked when they heard the front door close.

"Threats and bribery. Works every time."

"Is she likely to be back by eleven?" asked Van.

"She will be if she wants to go snowboarding tomorrow."

"Snowboarding? It's only September. In case you haven't noticed, there's no snow," Van said.

"We go to the indoor ski place near Wakefield."

"Oh, yeah. I've been there." Jamie said.

"Do you snowboard?" Van asked, surprise showing on her face.

"No. Skiing. But I haven't been for a while." Not since the preparation for the last skiing holiday with Sasha. But she didn't want to dwell on that. It had been shortly after that holiday that Sasha had gone. Had she already been carrying on with that woman? The thought had tortured Jamie during many a sleepless night. She hadn't noticed any change in her lover during their après-ski sessions, making love for hours at a time in the warmth of the hotel room, stimulated by the outdoor exercise, and what Jamie had thought was the passion of their love for each other.

Before she could wallow further in that unwanted memory, Laurel brought out dessert and Jamie groaned. She was already full but it was going to be hard to resist her hostess's homemade apple crumble with custard. It looked like she was going to have to head out for a night ride.

Chapter Two

Jamie nodded to the security guard as she pedalled past the car park barrier. He was busy checking out one of his monitors so just waved. She was thankful for that. Even after the exhilaration of her ride she wasn't ready for a hearty greeting of "All right, love." Asking him not to call her "love" wasn't an option either. She would normally just shoot him a quick smile before heading over to the rack to secure her bike. A blast of cold wind tugged at her backpack as she made her way up the steps, hurrying to get into the warmth and grab her first mug of coffee of the day.

Mike, the other technician, was already seated in front of his computer in the cramped space that doubled as the IT Services office and repair workshop. He glanced up at her from the Helpdesk emails that Jamie could see he was scrolling rapidly through. She placed her helmet on the stack of damaged keyboards behind the door.

"Coffee on, Mike?" she asked.

"It's brewing, love," he answered, giving her a sly grin.

"People have been killed for less, wise guy. Just make sure it's hot and black and on my desk when I get back."

She didn't wait for his standard crude response as she made her way down the hall to get changed in the toilet. Towelling off her hair, she looked in the mirror. There were more flecks of grey showing now, but she had to admit the dinner Friday evening at the Hope-Chambers residence had given her a boost. Sunday had been good as well. She'd gone for a long hike on the moors with one of her new Search and Rescue mates. Andy was great company and very knowledgeable about the area. He'd taken her under his wing when she'd applied to join the volunteer team shortly after moving to the town. Nearing the end of her six-month probationary period, she was looking forward to being able to participate in real life situations.

When she got back to the office, the coffee was on her desk but Mike had gone. There was a note stuck on her screen: "Sup up! Bring HP125A Cyan to LS10."

Taking a sip of the still hot coffee, she looked around. He must have been carrying something heavy if he couldn't manage one small printer toner. She located the right box, clipped her ID badge to her belt, and gulped down half the coffee. It was a shame to leave it but it would be cold by the time she reached the Lockside building on the other side of the canal.

Mike was lying on the floor in the corner of the room sorting through a mass of cables.

"What do they need that for?" she asked, staring at the monster-sized flat-screen television on the floor next to Mike's feet.

"No idea," he grunted. "Probably want a console next for playing games."

Jamie removed the new toner cartridge from its packaging and replaced the defunct one in the printer.

"They go through this stuff like water. What do they teach in here anyway?"

Mike sat up, having finally found the connection he needed. "E-learning."

"So, why do they have to print anything? Shouldn't it all be online?"

"Ah, the myth of the paperless office. Not likely to happen in my lifetime." That was a long time off considering he was half Jamie's age. "Remote's on the desk. Want to see what we can get on here."

Jamie picked up the remote and pressed the power button. "Great. Let's find out how the other half live. Jeremy Kyle's on now."

Mike raised his eyebrows. "How would you know that? I didn't think you watched TV."

She muted the sound on the set. "Had some time when I was made redundant, before I got this job. Seeing how other people have screwed up their lives made it worth getting out of bed in the morning." That was more information than Jamie had ever revealed to her co-worker before and he looked uncomfortable.

"Any sign of the boss?" he asked, tidying up the packaging.

"He wasn't in when I left."

Their team leader, as designated by HR, was becoming noticeably erratic with his timekeeping.

"Well, I don't know about you, but I'm getting fed up covering for him."

"Trouble at home, maybe."

"Maybe. But if he wants us to pick up the slack, he needs to let us in on it."

Sometimes Mike sounded wise beyond his years. But if Jonathan were having problems, she wasn't going to ask him. She didn't share her private life and could well understand if he wanted to keep things to himself. And if he was thinking of leaving, she had no doubt she could do his job. It would mean more money but she was actually enjoying just being a hands-on techie for a change. The extra money was hardly worth the hassle of having to write reports, attend meetings, and fill in forms. With the redundancy money from her last job, she had enough to get by. Purchasing the expensive road bike had been an investment in her health more than anything, both mental and physical.

"Hey, turn the sound up. It's the meerkats."

They watched the advert, laughing at the antics of the animated creatures. When it changed to a commercial for tampons, Mike declared the equipment roadworthy, telling Jamie to turn it off and leave the remote on the desk.

The rest of their day was busy and, if Mike hadn't reminded her, she would have forgotten to eat lunch again.

†

Van kept looking at her phone. She'd covered it with a file folder and wondered if she could get away with sending a text. Having wheedled Jamie's number out of Laurel, she'd spent a restless weekend and all day Monday wondering if she should call. The woman intrigued her. She kept seeing her brilliant smile and the way she absently brushed a hand through her hair when she was thinking. And there was her voice with its low, sexy timbre. But it couldn't have been developed through smoking; she seemed too sporty and health-conscious to have that vice.

Connor's head popped over the divider. "So how was it? The date?" He'd had Monday off so this was the first chance he'd had to quiz her.

"None of your business, pipsqueak."

"Come on. I've had three irate dickheads so far this morning that shouldn't be allowed to cross the road on their own, let alone operate a computer. I need some oral stimulation."

"I'll bet you do. But leave me out of it." She glanced at her screen. "I'll take this one, so you can go and get relief."

He stuck two fingers up at her and retreated to his side of the screen.

She got through six more sessions before she was able to take a break. Secreting her phone in her back pocket she made her way out to the car park. Fortunately, there were no smokers outside. Before she could chicken out again, she texted a quick message: *can u talk, van.* A direct phone call would have been easier but, knowing the nature of Jamie's job, she could be fixing something in a classroom full of students. And she probably wouldn't answer an unknown number.

Her phone vibrated in her hand and she jumped. Of course, she'd put it on silent while she had it on her desk. She held it up to her ear. "Hello."

"Van?"

It was definitely Jamie. That voice could make her tingle with just one syllable. "Yes."

"What do you want to talk about?"

Van's mind reeled and her carefully rehearsed speech disappeared. *Will you marry me?* No, that wasn't it. They hadn't had a proper first date yet.

"Van? Are you there?"

She focused on the third floor windows of the building opposite. "Um. Yes. Look, I left something at Laurel's so I'm popping over to collect it after work. Would you be free to meet me for a drink?" It sounded a bit flimsy, even to her. She held her breath, waiting for Jamie to answer.

"Okay. I'll meet you at the wine bar. Laurel knows where it is. Seven. Sorry, I've got to go."

"Great. See you later." But she was already gone.

Van smiled inanely to herself. Now she only had to let Laurel know.

Her friend's reaction wasn't what she'd expected. "It's bad enough having one hormonal teenager in the house."

"Well, it's your fault. You introduced us. I thought this was what you had in mind."

Laurel relented and gave her directions to the wine bar and an offer of a bed for the night if she didn't get invited back to Jamie's.

She arrived back at her desk smiling broadly. Now she just had to decide what to wear.

†

Wigan on a wet Tuesday evening—Phoebe Lemming wondered again why she had agreed to this reading. The three people scattered across the room looked like they had just come in to get out of the rain. To top it all, Sasha had managed to wriggle out of coming along. No support from her partner, again. At the start of their affair, Sasha would have come to her reading even if it had been in Siberia. What had happened in the last few months? They had moved into their dream house, finally, and she thought everything was perfect. Everything except the lack of Sasha's undivided attention. Maybe if she could find it in herself to be more affectionate towards the damn cat. As it was she could barely resist kicking it. The cat was a reminder of Sasha's past, an incarnation of her ex-girlfriend. She was jealous of the way Sasha held it, stroked it. Insane, she knew, but she couldn't help how she felt. Living too much inside her head wasn't good for her.

Meeting Sasha at the Manchester Literature Festival the year before had been a revelation. Past relationships faded into insignificance. It had been lust at first sight and Sasha had lived up to expectations. Now she felt she was losing her and it wasn't fair. She wanted Sasha, all of her.

Looking around the room she thought the reading might as well be taking place somewhere on the frozen steppes. The librarian gave her an encouraging smile, standing by the door as if expecting more punters to show up. The dozy woman had optimistically set out thirty chairs.

Phoebe glanced down at her notes. She hardly needed them, having given this talk dozens of times. She could even predict the questions she would be asked. *Where do you get your ideas from? How do you manage to write such realistically graphic murder scenes?'* Didn't these people watch the news? She didn't really have to make anything up.

The librarian gave her the nod to get started. Phoebe stood and moved to the lectern, placed her notes in front of her, and started to talk about her life of crime.

✝

Maddie had barely made it through the door when Laurel pounced.

"Guess what?"

She shrugged out of her coat and hung it up in the cupboard knowing she wasn't required to answer.

"The school phoned today. Tay's been skipping classes."

"That's hardly news."

"They're saying if her attendance doesn't improve, she'll be asked to leave."

"All right. I'll talk to her. But I need to have a shower first."

She spent more time under the water than normal, in no hurry to have another difficult conversation with their daughter. No matter how many books they'd both read on parenting, nothing really prepared them for this. But however hard the challenges of bringing up their two children, she didn't regret it for a minute. Her life had changed for the better from the moment she first saw Laurel.

It was at a friend's wedding, which she had reluctantly attended. The last thing she wanted to witness was someone else's happy day. Long-term relationships didn't seem like they were going to be part of her future any

31

time soon. Medical school, internships and starting out as a GP hadn't left much time for getting to know anyone. Laurel was playing piano at the reception as part of a duo. The other woman was the singer and had a magnificent voice, but it was watching Laurel's face and her hands as they danced over the keys that had her entranced. After several glasses of Champagne she worked up the courage to go over and make a request. For the life of her now she couldn't remember the name of the song she'd asked them to play. Laurel had looked up from the keyboard and smiled, and she'd been lost.

She was convinced that the pair must be lovers. They performed so well together. Then as they were packing up, once the bride and groom had gone, she heard the pianist tell the singer she would see her later in the week. And heard her name for the first time when the other woman responded: Laurel. If she hadn't been slightly drunk she was sure she would never have approached her. As it was, she managed to go over and introduce herself. Laurel accepted her invitation to meet her for a coffee the next day and that had been the start.

After their first year together they talked about having kids. Maddie had warned her that with the long hours she worked, she would be more like an absent dad at times. But Laurel had been happy with the arrangement. She was able to work from home while the children were at pre-school stage, and Maddie's mother living nearby helped with childcare arrangements in those early days. Leo was such a delight as a baby, and he was only one when Maddie decided she could take time off if necessary to give birth herself. They wanted him to have a brother or sister.

Their biggest decision had been about surnames for the children. Laurel's experience of working in a school had dissuaded them from the double-barrelled option. They decided on the compromise of giving them the surnames of their birth mothers. So they were christened respectively, Leo Chambers and Taylor Hope. Taylor was a family name they had decided they wanted to pass on. They couldn't have known when she was born that they would, in a few years' time, be constantly telling people she wasn't named after a female country singer. The connection pleased Tay now, though. Her friends thought the name was cool.

And now she was going to have to talk to the sixteen-year-old Taylor Hope who was showing all the signs of a rebellious teenager. This wasn't a trait that had come from her, so it had to be from the DNA of her unknown father. They had a photograph of a blond, blue-eyed young man, who had fit all their criteria for health and intelligence, but they didn't know anything else about him. The details of both male donors were in sealed envelopes in a locked drawer. Another thing she and Laurel had agreed on twenty years ago was that the identities of the children's fathers would remain hidden, until the time either of them asked.

†

Sasha looked around wondering where to start. First there had been the nightmare of the ring road in rush hour traffic and finding a place to park. All the university car parks were barrier controlled. Now she found herself in the midst of the campus without a clue where to start looking for Jamie. She didn't know if there would be a centralised IT Support or if they were allocated to faculties.

Her phone rang. It was Phoebe again, she knew without looking at the screen. She'd already had three missed calls from her. Sighing, she answered.

"Where the hell are you?"

"Nice to hear from you too."

"Don't play games with me, Sasha. I'm stuck in Wigan. No fucking trains for an hour at least. Come and get me."

Great. How to explain it would take her longer than an hour to get from Huddersfield to Wigan. "Sorry, babe. I can't leave yet. My next client's just arrived."

"At this time? Put them off. This is an emergency."

"Hardly. Get a taxi."

"Who's the client?"

"New author. You wouldn't know them."

"Try me. Must be good if you're seeing them now."

"Well, it's a first time novel, *The Moons of Septimus Seven*. But sci-fi's not really my thing. I'll have to let him down gently."

There was silence on the other end. Sasha thought she'd hung up. Finally she heard what sounded like a snort. "Fine, Alexandra. We'll talk about this when I get home." She disconnected abruptly. Sasha knew she was in serious trouble when Phoebe used her full name.

The campus was much larger than she'd expected. Sasha walked into the nearest building, needing to find a toilet if nothing else. After she'd relieved herself she had a brainwave. Of course, Jamie would probably drive here. She could have bought herself a new car with the redundancy payoff from her last job. As staff, she would be allowed in one of the controlled parking areas.

Sasha decided to try the nearest car park she could see, and set off down the steps to the security booth. The man inside was doing a Sudoku puzzle. Quickly. She admired his skill; she'd never got the hang of those. He looked up when she approached the window.

"Can I help you, love?"

"Yes. I'm looking for Jamie Steele. I think she usually parks here. Do you know if she's left yet?"

"Jamie Steele?" he tapped the pencil on the paper. "Oh, you've just missed her. She collected her bike half an hour ago."

"Her bike?"

"Yeah. She cycles in every day, rain or shine. Comes from somewhere over in the next valley, Hebden Bridge, I think. Must be nuts, but each to their own, eh, love?"

"Yes, you're absolutely right. Thanks."

Sasha made her way back to her car. It was a bit of a trek to the multi-story car park near the town hall but it gave her more time to think. Jamie on a bike. Unreal. She'd always been a keen hiker, but had never shown any interest in cycling. Maybe she'd been bitten by the Tour de France frenzy from the summer when the Tour had staged two sections of the Grand Depart in this part of Yorkshire. In fact, it had gone through Hebden Bridge she recalled, having seen the newspaper reports.

Seated in the car at last she looked at the clock on the dashboard. Choices. She could go home and face the music when a disgruntled Phoebe arrived back from Wigan, or she could drive over to Hebden Bridge and see if she could find Jamie. It wasn't a big place. Whatever she did, Phoebe was already pissed off. *Might as well be hung for a sheep as a lamb*, she thought, as she reprogrammed the Sat-Nav.

35

†

The ride had done nothing to settle the fluttering in her stomach. She could blame it on the egg salad sandwich Mike had thrust in front of her at three o'clock, but it was more likely the thought of what Van wanted from her. Meeting her for a drink was okay but she had the feeling Van wanted something more. Something she didn't feel she was ready for, yet, if ever.

A year and three days since Sasha left her. And she still couldn't block out images of their lovemaking. Waking up in the night, Jamie would reach for her, and be surprised, then alarmed to find an empty space. The despair would flare all over again. The utter finality of it all was now embodied in the sale of the house, the house they had bought together, the house where she thought they would grow old together. Whenever she thought of Sasha with the other woman it made her physically ill.

Stopping at a traffic light, she reached into her pack for an energy bar. The biggest climb was ahead of her, but once up that hill, she could coast down into the valley, and the final few miles into the town were on the level. However, today, feeling the need for a calmer environment, she slipped onto the canal towpath at Luddenden Foot and cycled the rest of the way breathing fresher air. In a few weeks it would be too dark at this time to use the path.

She reached the front door of the house and looking forward to a shower and a change of clothes before meeting up with Van. The body that detached itself from the side of the building startled her and she held the bike up in front of her face, ready to hurl it at the potential attacker.

"Whoa! Sorry to scare you."

It was Van standing there, hands up in surrender.

Jamie lowered the bike. "Uh. I thought we were meeting at the wine bar."

"Laurel gave me your address, and as I was early I thought I'd meet you here. Hope that's okay."

"Yeah, sure. I just need time to shower." Jamie decided she would need to have words with Laurel. Or maybe she should ask Maddie to talk to her.

"I've brought beer." Van held up a bag. "And they're cold."

What else had Laurel told her? Jamie wondered as she opened the door and led the way up the stairs to her attic hideaway.

✝

Van followed, enjoying the view of Jamie's well-toned lycra clad legs and butt as they climbed. Not many people could successfully carry off the lycra-look, but this woman rocked it. Out of breath by the time they reached the top, she promised herself she would start an exercise regime soon.

Once inside the room Jamie set her bike against one wall and unclipped the water bottle. She drank the remaining liquid and put the empty bottle on the floor.

"I'll hit the shower. There's a bottle opener on the bookcase."

The bookcase was something Van hadn't seen since her student days; two long roughhewn planks supported by bricks. She found the opener and popped the cap on both bottles. Looking around for a table, she was shocked to realise there wasn't one. An upturned plastic crate and a legless armchair by the windows at the far end of the long room were the only other bits of furniture. Jamie had disappeared behind a screen, which she guessed was where there might be a bed, possibly just a mattress if the rest of the minimal decor was anything to go by.

She took a swig of beer and crouched down to look at the books. Some computer manuals she recognised and a meagre selection of paperbacks that looked like they'd come from charity shops. She picked one up that she thought she'd read before.

The chair, once she'd lowered herself into it, was surprisingly comfortable. She balanced the beer bottle on the crate and opened the book. It was one she'd read some time ago. One of Felicity Lemon's early crime novels. She recalled that the clever twist at the end had left her feeling cheated. It was upsetting when the killer turned out to be either a cop involved in the investigation or a character that only showed up in the last thirty pages.

Jamie appeared again looking stunning in a pair of loose fitting jeans and red polo shirt. She picked up the other bottle of beer and joined Van by the window.

Van put the book down, sensing the other woman's discomfort. "Look, I'm sorry. I shouldn't have barged in on you like this."

"It's fine." Jamie ran her fingers through her still damp hair. An endearing habit Van thought she would never tire of seeing.

Jamie drank some of the beer, tipping her head back, giving Van a view of her strong neck muscles. She sipped at her own beer to distract herself from the hormonal urges that were building.

"You still okay with going to the wine bar? The only beer they have is bottled."

"Hey, your territory, your choice. I'm easy." *No doubt about that.*

"Right, well I like the food there and it'll be quiet at this time." She finished her beer and gave Van that smile; the one that melted her already softened insides. "Good to go."

Van struggled up from the chair, vowing once again that she would renew her gym membership.

It only took a few minutes to reach the centre of the town and Jamie led her along the same street she'd used when she walked from the train station. She hadn't noticed the wine bar even though she'd walked right past the entrance.

The downstairs rooms were fairly empty with only two couples sitting at tables. As Jamie had said, it was quiet.

The bartender greeted Jamie enthusiastically. This was clearly a regular haunt of hers. Jamie turned her head to ask, "Wine or beer?"

"Happy to share a red, if that's okay with you."

"Yeah. Good choice." She smiled at the bartender. "We'll be over there." She indicated one of the corner tables facing the bar.

"Does she know what you drink?" Van asked as they sat down.

"Yes, and what I eat. The menu selections are on the board up there."

Van glanced at the chalked menu choices listed above the bar. Mainly veggie options, she noted. "Are you a vegetarian?" She seemed to think Jamie had eaten her share of Laurel's *coq au vin* the other night.

"Most of the time. I don't eat much red meat, mostly chicken or fish. Although I won't say no to the odd bacon sandwich."

The friendly bartender arrived with two large globe glasses and a bottle of Barolo. She uncorked it at the table and poured a little for Jamie to taste. Jamie just smiled and told her to pour.

"Is it a special occasion?" Van asked as she watched the rich red wine flowing into her glass.

"No. But I'm past the stage of drinking the cheap stuff."

After taking their food orders, the bartender left them in peace. Jamie picked up her glass.

"Cheers. Thanks for inviting me out. Tuesday nights are usually a bit dull."

Van thought most nights must be dull for her, sitting alone in that sparsely furnished attic room without even a television for company. She decided to try a safe topic of conversation.

"So, you and Maddie were at uni together."

"Not exactly together. A med student wouldn't normally mix with a computer geek. We met through GaySoc, forerunner of today's LGBT society."

"What degree course did you do?"

"Computer Science, BSc. I was going to do the Masters but I got a job instead. In a bank. Working on security systems."

"Wow. So how come you're humping equipment around now?"

"I got made redundant from my last job. It was a real downer as I thought I was in line for promotion. And that was the time when my relationship broke up. So I just took the first job that came along. In a way, it's fine. I don't have to think much about what I'm doing and I like the physicality—not stuck in front of a screen all day."

"I can empathise with that. My job's pretty dull but I can't be arsed to look for anything else at the moment."

Their starters arrived and Van had another pang of self-awareness, watching Jamie start on her healthy-looking salad while she was faced with a plate of calorie-adding, fried goat cheese. Not a good choice.

"Do your parents live nearby?"

Jamie pushed an olive to the side of her plate. Without looking up she said, "No. They're divorced. Dad lives in Spain with his new wife, and my mother's in Bournemouth."

Van decided a psychology degree wasn't needed to know this wasn't a good subject to pursue. Asking further personal questions was evidently a potential minefield. Noticing the olives piling up on the edge of Jamie's plate, she plunged in. "If you don't want the olives, I'll eat them."

"Great. I forgot this salad came with them." She moved her plate across the table and deftly flicked the offending items onto Van's. "Do you see your parents?"

"We have regular family get-togethers—Christmas, birthdays, you know. They're in Chester, so it's not far to go. I'm an only child, so yeah, we're pretty close."

"That's nice."

Van couldn't read her expression as she studied a piece of lettuce forensically, as if expecting to find a slug lurking. Time to step onto safer ground. She started talking about a comedy programme and was relieved to find that Jamie had seen it, even without the benefit of a television set, courtesy of the catch up apps on her iPad. Van enjoyed seeing her smile, sometimes even laughing out loud, as they recalled their favourite scenes.

†

Sasha hadn't expected to be able to park her car so easily. The only other time she'd visited the town she remembered having to drive around several times before finding somewhere, and then hiking half a mile back into the centre. And she couldn't believe her next stroke of luck. Just as she pulled into the space, two women came around the corner. One was unmistakably Jamie. She watched them disappear between two large brown doors, a rather nondescript venue. She wasn't sure if it was the entrance to a bar or an apartment building.

The traffic out of Huddersfield had been heavy. She'd found herself in a long queue before she got anywhere near the turnoff that would take her onto the road leading towards Hebden Bridge. Roadworks on the Burnley Road had further delayed her. Still the timing couldn't have been better. She really hadn't worked out how she was going to find Jamie. The place wasn't that big but chances were high that she wouldn't have been going out on a Tuesday evening.

She unplugged her phone and was putting it into her bag when it rang and Phoebe's face lit up the screen. Not answering wasn't really an option. She decided to put on what she hoped sounded like a cheerfully innocent voice.

"Hi Feebs. Are you home now?"

"Yes. And where the hell are you? Do you have any idea what that taxi ride cost? We'll have to remortgage the house."

"Still in the meeting, babe. Just wrapping it up now."

"Great. I look forward to hearing how you got on with Felix." Her tone of voice indicated the opposite and Sasha knew she was in for a night of heavy grovelling.

Phoebe ended the call without saying anything else and Sasha sat back, closing her eyes. They snapped back open again. Wait, she hadn't given her the name of the author she was supposedly seeing. She shook her head. Maybe Phoebe knew him. They could have met at one of her readings or workshops. Maybe she'd even suggested he send his first novel to her.

Gathering herself together she opened the car door and stepped out onto the pavement. Crossing the road she saw the sign on the building and noted that it was a wine bar. The entrance didn't look particularly inviting. She hoped she wasn't descending into some dark den of iniquity. Who knew what Jamie was into now. Maybe in desperation she was visiting lap-dancing clubs.

Her fears were dispelled when she reached the bottom of the stairs. It just looked like a rather boring restaurant. Not many patrons. Jamie and the other woman weren't in the first room. She stopped before reaching the bar, spotting the back of Jamie's head.

Now that she was here and within range, Sasha really had no idea what she was going to say. *Sorry for ruining our life together, sweetheart.* Somehow she didn't think that would be a good start.

Jamie laughed at something the other woman said and Sasha's heart lurched. Did she really have any right to intrude on her ex's new life? She had taken so much away from her. Just because she was now unhappy with her choice, could she inflict more pain on the woman she had loved, and in the dark hours of the night, knew she still did?

✝

It was a relief to see that Van liked the food. Jamie wasn't sure she'd been keen on the menu options. The wine probably helped. The bottle was almost empty and they had only started eating their main courses. Van had a way of making her laugh and Jamie found she was enjoying the evening far more than she had thought she would. Relaxing into the warmth of her companion's smile and their shared laughter, she wasn't prepared for what happened next.

"Don't know if you want to look now, but there's a woman over there who's been staring at us for some time. I don't know anyone here apart from Laurel and Maddie, so she must be looking at you."

Jamie didn't turn around immediately. Other than the doctor and her wife, the only people she knew in the town were part of the Search and Rescue team. And any of them would just have come over to the table and said "hello."

"Oh, she's heading this way." Van put her fork down.

Jamie glanced around and found herself looking at the last person she would have expected to see there. She leapt up almost knocking over her wine glass.

"Sasha! What the fuck…?"

"Sorry. You've blocked my calls. I just needed to see you."

"Right. Tired of the new one already so you think you can waltz in and…"

Sasha held her hands up. She looked tired and worn down but Jamie's insides were churning.

"Stevie misses you."

"Don't you dare bring Stevie into this."

"Look, I'm sorry. This wasn't a good idea." She put a card on the table. "This is where I am now. Please, I would like to talk." She turned and walked away.

Jamie watched her go, and mumbled a hasty excuse to Van. She just made it to the toilet before she threw up. *Well, that was a waste of good wine.* After cleaning up, she returned to the table, somewhat surprised to see Van still there. She regained her seat, shakily.

There was a glass of water in front of her.

"Thought you might need that," Van was looking at her, eyes full of sympathy. "Who's Stevie?"

"Our cat." Jamie drank some water. "She took him, along with everything else."

They sat in silence for a few minutes. Jamie sipped at her water, trying to let the emotions wash through her. Finally she looked up at Van.

"I guess you think I'm stupid, getting wound up about a cat."

Van shrugged. "I wouldn't know. I've never owned one."

Jamie managed a thin smile. She pulled her phone out and scrolled through some photos. "You don't own cats, they own you." Finding the picture she wanted, she showed it to Van. "That's Stevie."

"Nice."

"Yeah." She looked at the close-up photo of the black cat's face, green eyes staring back at her, his expression of "feed me now!" that she could never resist.

Putting the phone away she looked at the half finished meal in front of her. "I'm sorry. I don't think I can eat this. If it's okay with you I'd like to leave now." She pulled her wallet out of her pocket and threw two twenties down. "That should cover it." Without a backward glance, she stood up and stumbled up the stairs and out onto the street. Van would think she was a pretty lousy date, but at the moment she couldn't get past the way Sasha had looked and the conflicting urges—the desire to lash out at her, or to fuck her senseless. Either wasn't a good feeling.

Back in her room she changed quickly into her riding gear and took the bike out. Adrenalin-fuelled, she made the lung-busting ride up to the reservoir in record time. The long climb was more of a workout than her muscles wanted after the day's rides to work and back, but she needed to exhaust herself before she could even think about trying to sleep that night.

✝

Van sat back in the easy chair and swirled the liquid around in her glass. Laurel had been surprised when she arrived back at the house before eight o'clock.

"What happened? Did she blow you off?"

"Not really. More like her ex showed up and freaked her out."

She refused to tell her the whole story until she was sitting down with a full glass of red wine and a plate of cheese and biscuits. By that time Maddie had joined them and wanted to hear all the gory details as well. Van finished the last of the cheese and warmed to her tale.

"We were getting on fine, I thought. Even though I'd showed up at her place and she didn't seem thrilled to see me. Well, I guess I hadn't thought that one through. Must have been a shock. Anyway, by the time we finished our starters I'd got her laughing and she seemed more relaxed.

We were just digging into our main courses when I noticed this woman watching us. She was definitely fixated on Jamie. When she eventually came over to our table, Jamie jumped up like a scalded cat."

"Wow! I wonder how she found her. Jamie says she's had no contact since they split up. And she'd told the solicitor handling the house sale that he wasn't to give her new address to Sasha." Laurel looked over at Maddie for confirmation.

"Could have been through work. Although Jamie got the job at the uni after Sasha left." Maddie sipped her own glass of wine, looking concerned. "How is Jamie now?"

"Not good. She threw up when this Sasha left."

"What! In the restaurant."

"No, she made it to the loo."

"Jesus! Maybe I should go see her."

"Somehow I don't think she'll appreciate a house call right now, doc. Looked like she just wanted to crawl off and lick her wounds."

"She's been doing that for the past year. It's not healthy."

"Yeah, well, she seemed more upset about the separation from their cat than anything. Even showed me a photo, like a proud parent."

Laurel snorted. "Oh yeah, we've all seen the photo of precious Stevie."

"Laurel! That's not kind." Maddie gave her partner a stern stare over her glasses. "Somehow I think she would have coped better with this whole thing if Sasha hadn't taken the cat with her."

†

47

It was after nine when Sasha got home, exhausted both physically and emotionally. Relaxing with a glass of chilled white wine and maybe a bath was what she really wanted. Instead she would be facing an irate Phoebe.

She made it as far as the kitchen before Phoebe appeared and started wanting answers. "Where the hell have you been? And I know it wasn't talking to Felix bloody LeMar."

Sasha opened the fridge and was dismayed to see there was no bottle of wine. She would have to settle for a beer. Luckily there was a Corona nestled between the pasta and the remnants of Sunday's chicken that she had planned to eat before her evening was derailed by the insane desire to see Jamie.

She brushed past a fuming Phoebe to locate the bottle opener in the cutlery drawer.

"I'm dog-tired, Feebs. Can't the interrogation wait?"

"No, it can't."

Sasha decided to try to defuse the unbridled anger aimed at her. "How was the reading?"

"Oh, wonderful. Wigan on a Tuesday evening. Three people and the librarian. And with the cost of a taxi added on, I'll be in debt until Christmas. Having a partner I could rely on for support would be nice." Phoebe's words dripped with sarcasm.

Sasha sighed. She gulped back some of the beer and walked through to the living room. Stevie was sprawled out on the sofa. She sat down next to him and stroked the black fur.

Phoebe followed her in and sat in the chair opposite. She leant forward, elbows on knees, eyes on full beam boring into Sasha.

"So, tell me. What did you think of Felix?"

"He's…um…very interesting."

"Really. Is that all you can say after spending, what, three hours with him?"

"Yeah, well, I'm still processing it."

Phoebe sat back, but the venomous glare betrayed her unconcealed anger. "Sash, you're full of shit!"

"Look, I'm sorry. I didn't think it would take so long." Stevie had woken up and was now kneading her lap and turning around in circles before settling down again. She stroked the top of his head and the purring increased. At least someone in the house was relaxed and happy.

"You weren't with Felix, so I would like to know where you were. Is that unreasonable?"

"How do you know I wasn't with Felix?" Sasha was surprised to find she'd finished the beer. She wanted to get another one but disturbing Stevie when he'd just got resettled wasn't an option.

"Really, Sasha, you can be a bit dim sometimes. Didn't the name ring any bells with you?"

Sasha closed her eyes. The name, Felix LeMar. Her eyes popped open. "Oh, fuck. Since when did you start writing science fiction?" Phoebe's pen name for her crime books was Felicity Lemon. Yes, she should have twigged.

"Since crime isn't paying that well at the moment. So, are you really interested in *Septimus Seven*?"

"No. I only read three pages and tossed it straight into the slush pile."

Phoebe stood up. Sasha braced herself for the assault. Criticising her lover's work was the ultimate weapon of mass destruction to their relationship. Having an affair, which is what Phoebe thought she had been doing that evening, was secondary.

"I'm going to bed. You can sleep with the cat since you seem to think more of him than you do me." She stalked out of the room and Sasha heard the heavy footsteps climb the stairs ending with a hard slam of the bedroom door.

✝

The business card stared up at her from the window ledge where she'd left it. Sasha still worked for Smoke Rising Publishing, or SRP as they styled themselves now. Jamie knew that. But Sasha had neatly printed out her home address, email, and phone numbers on the back. An address she recognised, only a few miles from where they'd lived together. She wondered if Stevie had found it hard to make the adjustment, if he'd ever wandered off to look for their old home. Visions of his face staring out from posters on lampposts and bus shelters haunted her. She shuddered.

The last thing she had expected, Sasha stalking her. It had all been so final when she left. Their last contact had been a few months later, just when Jamie was starting to feel she could face the world each day without bursting into tears, arriving home to find Sasha seated on the living room floor raking through the CDs with a selection of DVDs already piled up next to her. The words they shared on that occasion had not been amicable.

Sasha hadn't told her anything about the other woman. Jamie only found out from a mutual friend who seemed to think she needed to know all the gory details. "Phoebe Lemming. I mean, what kind of name is that? She's a writer, you know. Has a ridiculous pseudonym as well, Felicity Lemon. Honestly, you'd think a writer could come up with something better."

It made sense that the woman was a writer. Sasha would have met her through her work. She'd scoured the SRP website and hadn't found any Lemon books. A search on Amazon revealed the name of her publisher and a small photo on her author profile. So, Sasha must have met her at some literary event, one of those boring book festivals Jamie always found an excuse not to attend. Jamie couldn't gauge what the attraction was from that one photo. She thought the woman's eyes were too close together. The smile looked false as well, too many teeth. And according to her bio she was only thirty-nine. Somehow Jamie doubted that was true. Another fiction. Curiosity got the better of her when she found a Felicity Lemon novel in a charity shop. She'd tried reading it but couldn't get into the story. All she could see was an image of Sasha in bed with another woman, with the writer's face and a Pamela Anderson body.

Alexandra Imogen Elizabeth Fairfield. She should have known better than to hook up with someone with a public school background and two middle names. She didn't even have one. Her mother, disappointed that she wasn't a boy, had named her Jamie. Just Jamie. It wasn't a nickname or a family name. When her brother was born five years later, he had been graced with a first and a middle name.

Sasha's friends had always looked down on her. She'd overheard more than a few disparaging remarks at dinner parties when the speakers had commented on why Sasha was with her when she could have the pick of anyone. So Jamie couldn't join in with their pretentious talk about the books they'd read and the plays they'd seen. But they were quite happy to call on her services when anything went wrong with their computers.

Only nine o'clock. The turmoil she'd felt on seeing Sasha in the wine bar had settled down to a dull ache, a familiar tightness in her chest. The bike ride had restored her appetite, though. Deciding it might be a good idea to see if she could hold down some food, she ventured out into the town again. Things were just starting to liven up. School age kids who should have been at home doing homework were gathered in the usual spots. She walked past a group of scantily clad girls and then backed up.

"Taylor?"

The girl with the least amount of clothing on and the most make up stared at her. And smiled in recognition. "Hey, James. Good to see you." She peeled herself away from her mates and took Jamie by the arm. "Come on. You owe me a drink."

Jamie let herself be led away from the group. She stopped when they were out of earshot and looked at the youngster. "I'm guessing you didn't leave the house looking like this."

"Turns you on, does it?" Tay batted her false eyelashes at Jamie. One of them looked like it was about to fall off.

"I'm not interested in little girls. But if you want my opinion, you look better without the makeup and the trashy outfit."

Taylor pouted at her. "Well if you're going to be mean you can at least buy me a drink."

"You're underage, so if I did buy you one, it would be non alcoholic."

The girl's expression changed to one of concern. "You're not going to rat me out, are you?"

"Wouldn't dream of it." Jamie smiled at her. "Go on, have fun with your mates."

She walked away and headed for the Italian restaurant in the old mill. If it was too busy to fit her in, she could always get a takeaway pizza. When she looked back from the doorway, Taylor's group had disappeared. Did her parents need to know what she was doing? She shook her head. Her intervention wouldn't make a blind bit of difference. They were kids doing what kids did. At sixteen she wouldn't have appreciated some old bat giving her grief about the way she dressed or acted.

Chapter Three

The early morning train into Manchester was packed. Van knew she should have left Laurel's earlier if she'd wanted to get a seat. The misleadingly named TransPennine Express consisted of three elderly carriages. They seriously needed to upgrade their rolling stock. With the number of passengers on this route, the company had to be coining it.

Sleep hadn't come easily the night before. They hadn't stayed up late, and it wasn't the amount of wine she drank, it was Jamie's face when the ex-from-hell showed up. She wondered what Jamie had done after they parted ways outside the wine bar. It was depressing to think of the sparsely furnished attic room Jamie was going back to. Most student digs were more lavishly appointed these days. They even had free Wi-Fi in on-campus accommodation.

Her phone started up with "The March of the Penguins." She grabbed it from her bag and saw she had a text message from the object of her thoughts. Leaning back into the luggage rack as the train lurched to one side, she opened it up.

Soz abt lst nite. Do u wnt 2 try again?

Soz! Honestly, the woman was forty-nine. Still, it made her smile. Yes, she wanted to try again. Why give up on a first date just because she threw up in the toilet? At least it hadn't been because of her.

She texted back. *Sure. Fri ok?*

By the time the train reached Victoria Station they had exchanged five more texts and agreed on a time and place. Van was relieved she wanted to meet up in Manchester. She figured her welcome was wearing out at Laurel's. Two overnight stays in the space of five days hadn't gone down well with the doctor. Maddie was always polite to her, but she knew she was mainly tolerated as an old friend of Laurel's.

The next three days were going to drag. She was looking forward to seeing Jamie again even if she wasn't completely over her ex. Van had to admit that Sasha, even in the dim light of the bar, was an attractive woman. Dark, auburn-highlighted hair sweeping her shoulders, slim and slightly shorter than Jamie, but with a few more curves.

Stopping at the coffee vendors stall, she decided on an Americano rather than her usual full fat latte. How many pounds could she shed before Friday?

✝

Maddie leant against the breakfast bar watching Laurel pack a lunch for Taylor.

"I don't know why you bother. You know she doesn't eat those. I bet she trades it for smokes."

"She doesn't smoke."

"I've smelt it on her. I can assure you she does." Maddie knew that the anti-smoking messages she'd given both the children would have made little difference in Taylor's case. She could only hope that it was a passing fad, not something that would become an ingrained habit with her daughter. Seeing her father die a painfully slow death from lung cancer at the age of thirty-seven had been her motivation at the tender age of twelve for becoming a doctor.

She took another sip of the rapidly cooling coffee. "Anyway, she's in sixth form now. It isn't cool to take a packed lunch. She probably dumps it before reaching the bus stop."

Maddie paused, aware of a stifled sob from her wife. She put her mug down and opened her arms. "Hey, sweetheart."

Laurel turned from the counter and stepped into her embrace. Without shoes on, they were almost the same height and Maddie only had to tilt her head up slightly to reach Laurel's lips. She kissed her lightly before pulling back to ask, "What is it?"

"I just want to feel some connection with her. She doesn't talk to me anymore."

"It's a phase. Being a teenager. Who would want to go through that again?" She held onto Laurel, waiting for her to calm down. "Look, once Leo's gone, we'll spend some time with her together."

"Leo." Laurel stepped away and gave her a weak smile. "Hard to believe our baby boy's going off to uni."

Maddie looked into her eyes. There it was. The reality of Leo being away from home for the first time, that was the real reason for the emotional outburst.

"Are you okay with driving him over to Keele tomorrow? I'm sorry I can't go with you but I've got a full day with Neil being off sick. We haven't been able to get a locum to cover."

Laurel nodded.

"He'll only be two hours away. He can come home any time he wants. But we have to let him find his feet." Even as she spoke the words, Maddie knew Laurel wasn't really listening.

"It's just…well, you know. I don't think he has any practical skills. Like feeding himself. Getting out of bed in time for his classes without some encouragement."

"It's high time he learned. And the only way he's going to do that is by having to do it himself."

Laurel just nodded again and turned back to the counter to finish packing Taylor's lunch.

This was an old argument. Maddie had been trying for a long time to get Laurel to see she wasn't doing their son any favours by mollycoddling him through his teenage years. It wasn't any wonder their daughter felt left out at times. Leo and Laurel had always shared a special connection, which may have been because she was his birth mother but also because of their keen interests in music and mathematics. Maddie knew that Laurel loved Taylor just as much as Leo but there was always a tension between them these days. Tay knew which buttons to press and Laurel reacted predictably. Once Leo was settled into his accommodation at Keele, she promised herself that she would take a break from work to spend some quality time with both Laurel and Taylor, two of the three most important women in her life.

"What's Leo doing today?" she asked.

"He's going over to see Nan and then catching up with a few of his mates. He's taken my car."

"He could have taken the bus." Another win for Leo. Maddie was sure that even if Tay passed her driving test first time, Laurel wouldn't be letting her take her car anywhere. "I hope you warned him not to drink and drive."

"He would never do that."

He's an eighteen-year-old boy driving a nearly new Ford Focus, the car of choice for boy racers, Maddie thought. Sensible as he undoubtedly was for his age, what young man could resist showing off to his mates given the chance?

Maddie shook her head. She would call her mother when she got to work to reinforce the drink drive message. Nan spoiled Leo almost as much as Laurel but she would be concerned for his safety as well.

"I'll be off now. See you later, love." Maddie picked up her medical bag and walked quickly down the hall.

†

Laurel heard the door slam and held onto the counter. Part of her knew Maddie was right. She shouldn't have let Leo take the car but she wasn't able to resist his smile. And to have him venture out of his room that early in the day was so unusual she had given in straight away. She had made him promise to be home by six. It was his last evening at home before leaving for his first term at university and she was planning to make his favourite meal for him. The main course was simple—steak and chips with grilled tomatoes on the side. No salad. He was okay with cooked vegetables, apart from broccoli, but she hadn't succeeded in getting him to eat salad. And for dessert she was making a rich chocolate mousse with whipped cream and maraschino cherries on top. Tay wouldn't eat any cherries as she believed the story Maddie had told her that these cherries were so full of chemicals they didn't dissolve easily and stayed in your intestines for seven years. She would have to cook fishcakes for Maddie and Taylor. A full-size steak would be wasted on them.

And now she was without the car, she would be making the trip to the supermarket in Halifax on the bus. Even though Maddie's vehicle was likely to be sitting in the surgery car park all day, she couldn't ask to use it. Maybe she should abandon the idea of cooking and just take them all out to their favourite local Italian restaurant. Leo could still have his steak and the others would have a wider choice from the menu.

She smiled. Yes, that was a better idea. She could relax and just make a final check in Leo's room to make sure he'd packed everything he would need. She had already made up a food hamper for him.

"Hey, momma bear, what's cooking?"

Laurel looked round at her daughter who had bounced into the room wearing what looked like a pantomime costume. God, she missed the days when all she had to worry about was the length of her uniform skirt. There seemed to be no dress code whatsoever at the school's sixth form. She wished they had forced Tay to make an effort to apply to one of the colleges in Huddersfield. Like so many of her peers though she had opted for the easy option, staying at the local high school where she was familiar with the environment and the staff.

"You're not wearing that to school, are you?"

"No, of course not. I just thought I would put it on to wind you up." Taylor's sarcastic tone made Laurel want to slap her. She bit back an angry response. That was what the girl wanted.

"Here's your lunch."

Taylor poured herself an orange juice and looked at the brown bag sitting on the counter. "You don't have to make me lunch, you know. I'm not ten anymore. Five quid would see me right for the day."

"This is healthier than anything you could buy."

"Jeez, mum. Nobody I know takes a packed lunch. That is so primary school. Give me a break."

Laurel remembered what Maddie had said the other night about bribery. "Okay. So if I give you a fiver, will you change into something I consider more acceptable for wearing to school?"

Taylor grinned. "Yeah. Magic." She made a quick about turn and raced back up the stairs.

Laurel closed her eyes and wondered what she had let herself in for. Five pounds a day would turn into twenty-five pounds a week. Plus there was whatever cash Maddie slipped to the girl when she wasn't looking. An experienced blackmailer didn't have anything on their daughter.

She opened her eyes again when Taylor appeared back in the kitchen.

"Is this okay?"

A check shirt tucked into a pair of not very tight jeans. Laurel couldn't help thinking that Taylor looked like a baby dyke and a very attractive one at that. Her hair was tied back in a ponytail and she wasn't wearing any makeup. She wondered why she hadn't noticed it before. Tay had a lot of friends of both sexes, but she'd never gone out on dates with any one person. She'd never mentioned anyone special. But at that age, and with the stand-off relationship they had, she wasn't likely to tell Laurel if there was anyone.

"Mum? Is this okay?"

"Yes, love. That's great." Laurel found her handbag and rooted out a five-pound note. "Here you go. And don't make any plans for tonight. We're all going out for dinner."

"Oh, yeah. Of course, Leo's last night." She took the fiver and tucked it into a back pocket before swaggering off down the hall.

Damn, she even has the walk. Laurel thought she should talk to Maddie about this at the first opportunity.

†

The manuscript stared up at her accusingly. Sasha took a deep breath and riffled through the pages. Was it worth giving it a try to save her relationship? Was her relationship worth saving? Thoughts of Jamie had consumed all her energy the last few weeks.

Stevie climbed up onto her lap and kneaded the tops of her legs before settling down. She stroked his head until he settled into a contented purr. She sometimes thought he knew when she was thinking of her ex-lover.

She stopped on one of the pages and looked down at the words. Words carefully crafted by her current lover.

Turning from the burial site, she shuffled down the grassy path to the wide-open space of the meadow. A few lizards lay out on the large rocks, sunning contentedly. Morgana walked up to the largest one, a gorgeous golden green, and ten feet long. She stroked the soft spot above its eyes.

"Well, my pretty, it's time for our meal. A hearty soup today, made from tree roots."

The lizard yawned, its massive row of shining teeth an impressive sight. Morgana waited a moment, her head on one side before forming the words. "Come along when you're ready."

She walked across the clearing to her crude shelter. The lizards, she reflected, were growing at an incredible rate...several inches a day some of them. They spoke to her as their capacity for communication grew too, speaking silently into her mind. Two in the meadow had become her constant companions, youngsters by lizard standards. They had appeared not long after her own arrival in this place, drawn perhaps by the small colony of their own kind. She had learned their names but they told her nothing of whence they came. Rhiannon and Gwydion. They did, however, tell her much of the new world for they had witnessed many of Hera's changes.

They introduced Morgana to the word 'dragon'. She had felt her toes go numb when she first heard it. Her mind whirled as a vista of dragon worlds opened up to her...a multitude of images crowded in from all the lizards in the colony, causing explosions in parts of her brain previously unused.

The dragons, they told her, were awakening!

For fuck's sake, Morgana and dragons! Sasha put the page down and sighed. Stevie raised his head to look at her.

"Yes, Stevie, your Aunt Phoebe has lost the plot." There was no way she could even consider trying to flog this crap to her usual publishing contacts. Sasha had a reputation to uphold.

Picking the cat up in one hand and the manuscript in the other, she marched across the hall and put the wad of paper on Phoebe's desk, thankful that it would be a few hours before the writer got home and she would have to face more of her baleful looks.

†

Jamie walked down Dean Street, noting how little had changed since she'd last been on the busy thoroughfare through the heart of the city. Van was waiting outside the tapas restaurant they'd agreed on. It wasn't one that had any association with Sasha. She'd only been there with her former work colleagues.

"Hi, have you been waiting long?"

"No, I just got here."

Somehow Jamie knew that wasn't true. British people didn't balk at telling white lies if it meant not having to say what they really thought. In this case, *you're ten minutes late, I thought you weren't coming.*

"Well I'll try not to throw up on you this time."

"Okay. I'll hold you to that."

Once inside the restaurant they were shown to a table for two by the window. It took a bit of negotiation but they eventually managed to order a selection of tapas dishes. The waiter brought bread and a bowl of olives with their drinks. Jamie had decided to stick with beer for the evening and ordered a bottle of Desperados. Van was drinking white wine. It seemed, after their experience earlier in the week, red wine was out of favour.

Relaxing into the warm atmosphere of the Spanish restaurant, Jamie found herself enjoying Van's company again. They'd covered a number of neutral topics starting with the weather, moving on to computer programmes. They'd already talked about the one comedy show they'd both watched the last time they met. But online gaming was another matter. Jamie admitted to not being attracted to console games but liked touchscreen apps like *Angry Birds* and *Super Stickman Golf*. Van was more into *Call of Duty* and *Grand Theft Auto*.

"That's teenage boy stuff," Jamie told her.

"Get lost. I'm usually playing against thirty-five year olds. And gender doesn't come into it."

After the meal, they wandered out onto the street and Van asked if she would like to come back to her flat for coffee.

"Is it far?"

"No, we can walk there."

"Really. How'd you get a place in the city centre?"

"Would you believe that I'm an international drug dealer?"

"No."

"How about the bank of Mum and Dad?"

"That's more like it. Are you still paying off the mortgage?"

"Yeah. I'll be in debt until I'm ninety. But I love it."

When they reached the apartment block near the Oxford Street Station, Jamie could see why. It was a modern building and the views from Van's flat on the tenth floor were stunning. She was hit with pangs of nostalgia from her years of working in Manchester.

Van went into the kitchen to make coffee and told Jamie to choose some music from her player. The living room was furnished with more gadgets than a Dixon's outlet. The widescreen television took up most of one wall, the latest HD smart TV. The recliner facing it had the remote and games controller handily placed on the armrests.

She tapped the menu on the iPod sitting in the Bose sound dock. Small Bluetooth-connected speakers were situated in each corner of the room. The music selection wasn't entirely to her taste but she found a Lily Allen album she recognised and started it playing.

"Hey, good choice," Van said, emerging from the kitchen with two mugs of coffee. "Her lyrics always make me laugh."

"Yeah, me too."

Jamie sipped her coffee and wondered how she was going to approach her request with Van. As if reading her mind, Van brought the subject up. The elephant that had been with them all evening.

"Look, promise not to throw up. But I couldn't help wondering, why do you think Sasha wanted to see you?"

"I really don't know. I haven't seen her in nine months."

"How long were you together?"

"Six years. I guess she got the seven year itch early."

"Wow. That really sucks."

"Tell me about it."

"I'm sorry, Jamie. I shouldn't have mentioned it."

"It's okay. You were there." Jamie took a deep breath. "Look, I know it's a lot to ask. But, would you mind if I stayed here tonight? I thought I'd go over to Bury tomorrow, and it would be an easier journey from here."

Van took a large gulp of coffee. Jamie could tell she knew she wasn't asking to sleep with her. After a moment's silence while Lily's voice intoned, "It's hard out here...for a bitch," Van nodded. "Yeah, sure. I've got a spare room."

Jamie smiled at her, relieved. "Thanks, I appreciate it. Now, are you going to show me how to play a game on that thing." She nodded at the TV screen.

✝

It took all her powers of persuasion to get Jamie to have breakfast before she set off. She'd said she would grab a coffee on her way to the tram stop, but Van convinced her that getting some toast inside her would help. Even though she wasn't sure what it would help with. Jamie hadn't been forthcoming about her plans for the day, but if Van had to guess, it was something to do with the visit from her ex. Of course she had looked at the card the woman left when Jamie shot off to the toilet. Alexandra Fairfield. How did you get "Sasha" from that? Her parents must have been reading the same Russian novels as hers. The address she'd handwritten on the back of the business card was in Bury.

The night before, Van lay awake in her bed achingly aware of Jamie's presence in the next room. The whole evening had been pure torture. Every smile, every gesture, burned into her memory. And when they had been playing the game, their hands sometimes touching, she had thought she would lose it completely and make a grab for the woman.

Behave yourself, Van, she'd admonished herself more than once. *She's not interested.* For now it looked like she was going to have to settle for a developing friendship. If Jamie needed a shoulder to cry on, she could be there for her.

Although it would suck big time if that were to be the only intimacy that ever happened between them.

†

Phoebe still wasn't speaking to her. She'd got up early and gone into her den to write. When she emerged an hour later looking for more coffee, Sasha had been sitting at the kitchen table eating cereal and reading the paper on her iPad.

Mid-morning Phoebe muttered something about shopping and slammed the front door on the way out. Sasha looked over at Stevie who was snoozing on the chair by the window. He seemed content. But he hadn't had four nights of the cold shoulder from his lover. Living with a writer was turning out to be hard work. Phoebe's personality seemed to have undergone a complete change from when they first met. Sasha was starting to feel that she had been used. Had Phoebe targeted her, thinking she could help with her career? That was so wrong, on so many levels. Sasha had to ask herself, again, why she had been so quick to abandon Jamie. Their life together hadn't been that bad. In fact, it had been good in many ways. What did Phoebe have that Jamie didn't? There was no comparison. They were two totally different people. She couldn't have found someone so completely the opposite of Jamie if she'd been consciously looking. *Had she been unconsciously looking?*

Sasha was startled out of her reverie by a knock on the door. It was too early for the post and she wasn't expecting a parcel.

"Jamie!"

"Can I come in?"

67

"Yes, of course." Sasha stepped aside.

"Is she out?"

"Yes, but I don't know when she'll be back."

Jamie wandered into the living room and Sasha followed.

"Nice place."

Sasha watched as Jamie took in the elegant matching furniture and decor. All chosen by Phoebe. Stevie was awake and eyeing them warily. Jamie hadn't noticed him, she was staring at the picture over the fireplace.

"I can't believe you kept this."

It was a painting they had bought together. By the artist who always managed to place a black cat somewhere in the image. Sasha watched Jamie as she put her hand out to where the cat could just be seen in one of the old factory windows.

Stevie had jumped off the chair and was now looking up at Jamie. He started winding his body through her legs and meowing. The reunion was painful to watch as Jamie scooped him up into her arms, cradling him like a baby. She bent her head towards his and he licked her face. If cats could smile, that's what he was doing and the purr was louder than any she'd heard from him before.

"I told you he's missed you."

"Not as much as I've missed him."

"Is that why you came?"

"Yes." Jamie's voice was muffled as her face was buried in the cat's fur.

Sasha was sure Jamie was crying; she felt close to tears herself. The next words that came out of her mouth surprised her.

"Look. Phoebe doesn't really like having him here. Why don't you take him back with you?"

Jamie looked at her, eyes glistening. Sasha wanted to hold her. The only other times she'd ever seen Jamie cry was on the anniversary of her brother's death in Afghanistan. Two occasions each year—the date in August when the family received the news, and Remembrance Day on the eleventh of November.

"I don't have a garden."

"That's okay. He's a house cat now. Just after we moved here he went missing. Found his way back to our old place. A neighbour found him sitting on the doorstep. Luckily she remembered where I worked."

"I dreamt about that. About him being missing." The tears were flowing freely now.

Oh, God, Jamie. Sasha wanted desperately to make it up to her. Jamie had been her rock for so many years and she had just thoughtlessly thrown her away. For what? Lust-filled encounters that had seemed fun and exciting at the time. Trapped now in a fiction of her own making.

"I'll get his things together. I can drive you over." She busied herself finding Stevie's toys, his bed, favourite blanket. She packed up the litter tray, bags of extra litter, and tins of food.

When she came back from putting everything in the car, Jamie was leaning back in the recliner with Stevie resting on her chest. Both had their eyes closed. The cat was purring loudly and Sasha thought maybe Jamie was as well.

She held out the travel basket. "Ready to go. If you put him in here, we can set off now."

Jamie opened her eyes and looked up at her. "I can't put him in there. He'll think we're going to see the vet. I'll hold him."

"Okay. Well, we'll take it with us. You may need it sometime."

With Jamie still holding tightly to Stevie, she led the way out to her car. She put the basket in the boot with the other things.

"What about his scratching post?"

"Um, it got lost in the move."

Jamie gave her a look that Sasha recognised only too well. "You mean, she didn't want it here, in her *Homes and Gardens* house."

Sasha shrugged. She really didn't want to get into a slanging match with her ex concerning her current lover.

Putting the radio on in the car, they listened to the Saturday morning programme playing *Sounds of the Sixties*. The soothing tones of the presenter, Brian Matthews, and the anodyne love songs of the period, filled the silence between them. Stevie curled up in Jamie's lap and slept through the entire journey.

†

Jamie closed her eyes against the late afternoon sun reaching her through the attic windows. The events of the day seemed surreal now. Stevie had settled in to his new surroundings without fuss. After a quick inspection of the room, he took over the chair and made himself comfortable. She leant back against the wall, stretching her legs out along the floor.

Sasha hadn't stayed long. Finding a parking spot anywhere near the house on a Saturday lunchtime wasn't possible so she'd had to leave the car on a double yellow line and hope the town's diligent traffic warden was busy elsewhere. Sasha carried all the stuff from the car, making several trips while Jamie introduced Stevie to his new home. She had noted the shock on Sasha's face when she saw the lack of furnishings in her room.

"Stevie's got more stuff than you. Have you just moved in?"

"No. I've been here for six months. It's cheap and it's a great location, handy for everything."

When she'd gone, Jamie looked around. Sasha was right. Stevie's possessions did seem to fill the place up. He wasn't likely to use the cat bed. His favoured spot had been curled up on the pillow next to Jamie's face. But Sasha had insisted he used the bed. Well, the home wrecker wouldn't have wanted him anywhere near her no doubt perfect bedroom suite. She was surprised Stevie had even been allowed in the living room, but maybe that only happened when Miss *Country Living* was out of the house.

She would have to get him a scratching post. The one they'd had was just a simple post, but looking online she found a wide range of elaborate structures that would give him some necessary exercise. He would need something to amuse himself during the hours she was out at work.

Jamie looked over at the sleeping cat. "Just you and me now, buddy." Smiling to herself, she clicked the "buy" option for a cat tree on her iPad. "We'll be fine."

She almost believed it.

Chapter Four

Pacing around the small room, Phoebe looked over at her blank computer screen and felt the despair hit her hard again. Writer's block. Everyone suffered from it at times. Usually her tried and true methods got her past it—a few days of anguish at the most before the words started to flow once more. This time nothing was working—not sitting in her favourite coffee shop, watching people, listening to snatches of conversation; not going into the city and browsing the shelves in Waterstones while trying not to feel depressed that the bookshop had removed the apostrophe from its name.

The root of the problem, Phoebe knew, was Sasha. Their arguments had been getting more and more heated. And since the night she'd got home from Wigan they hadn't slept together. Her anger had only increased when she arrived home on Saturday to find both Sasha and the damned cat gone. Sasha returned eventually and told her about her ex's visit and her spur of the moment decision to let her take the cat.

Well, she didn't miss the cat. But the thought that Sasha had reconnected in any way with Jamie was disturbing. Was that where she had been on the night she'd told her she was with the fictional Felix LeMar? It still hurt that Sasha had lied so blatantly. If she'd picked another author's name, Phoebe wouldn't have been any the wiser. But the recognition had been building for some time that their relationship wasn't what it had been in the beginning. Sasha had been growing distant and harder to reach.

She had never met Jamie Steele, but from the photo that had been on Sasha's desk the first time Phoebe walked into her office, there was nothing attractive about her. A sickly sort of smile, puppy-dog brown eyes, nondescript, short brown hair. The kind of character in her crime novels who would have been killed off in the first chapter, not because they'd done anything vile, but because they had witnessed something they shouldn't—an innocent bystander who becomes a victim. But these victims were supposed to lie down and stay dead. Jamie seemed to have resurrected herself in Sasha's mind. This wasn't good. Sasha was hers now and she planned to keep her.

From the very first time she'd seen Sasha at the Festival she knew she wanted her. She had been signing books for an hour, but the waiting line had dwindled down to the last few. Phoebe managed to keep her smile in place as she signed, but kept looking over to make sure the woman she had her eye on was still there.

"Just taking a break," she said to the author next to her when the last person in her queue had walked off.

Sasha was talking to a tall man who was a sales rep for one of the big houses. The man moved away as she approached so she was able to make it look like a casual meeting.

"Hi. I don't think I've seen you here before." Not one of the best pick-up lines she could have opened with, but she wasn't used to feeling this nervous.

The woman smiled and Phoebe was instantly lost for words.

"Well, I've seen you. Felicity Lemon, right?"

"Yes. But that's not my real name. It's a pen name."

"I thought it might be." That charming smile again. And lovely hazel eyes. Her hair, resting on her shoulders, might have been brown once but was now streaked with auburn highlights. She held out her hand. "Sasha Fairfield. I'm with SRP."

And that, as they say, was that. Phoebe asked if she had any plans for dinner. A hastily consumed meal was followed by a night of passion in Phoebe's hotel room. For some months they met once a week, sometimes only managing an afternoon when Sasha could make plausible excuses for not being in her office. Although Sasha wasn't forthcoming about her private life, Phoebe suspected there was someone else. Eventually she demanded Sasha make a choice. If Sasha was going to be with her, Phoebe wanted all of her. At the time she didn't think the other person in her lover's life could be very important. Sasha didn't hesitate in agreeing to move in with her, only asking if she could bring the cat.

The manuscript sat on the desk, looking up at her accusingly. Rejected by Sasha. Well, it was SRP's loss. She would send it to another agent, one who knew something about fantasy and sci-fi. *The Moons of Septimus Seven* was too good a book to languish in a slush pile. Regardless of what Sasha thought of it, Phoebe was determined to get it out into circulation again.

Now she only had to form an action plan to re-ignite Sasha's passion for her. She knew it was there, just dormant. But she needed to do something. She wanted Sasha back in her bed. Once those juices started flowing, she was sure the words would come back as well.

✝

Maddie turned the letter over in her hands. She'd retrieved it from the outgoing mail tray and wondered now what she was going to do. It was never good to be emotionally involved with patients. An "abnormal result" didn't necessarily mean there was a major problem, though. These initial screenings weren't always accurate. Another test would clarify the situation. But how was she going to explain that to this particular patient without sending her into a panic?

Finally she picked up her mobile and phoned home. No answer. Laurel was probably with a student.

She left a message. "Hi sweetie. Just one more house call to make. See you soon."

Leaving the Freelander in the Surgery car park, she walked up the narrow street to Jamie's residence. The steepness of the climb didn't bother her. You couldn't live in Hebden Bridge and avoid uphill walks. The steps up to the attic room were a killer though. She stopped at the door and caught her breath before knocking. Perhaps she should have phoned ahead to make sure her patient was home.

"Come in."

Jamie would know it was a friend. She didn't give the front door security code out to everyone.

Maddie opened the door and was immediately struck by the changes. The place almost looked furnished compared to the last time she'd visited. A three-seater sofa under the window replaced the legless armchair, although the chair was still there and occupied by a large black cat. Jamie looked up from her iPad, long legs stretched out from her reclining position on the new addition to the room.

"Finally splashed out on some furniture, I see." Maddie smiled.

"Not really. A guilt offering from Sasha. Although it's probably Stevie's comfort she's worried about, not mine."

"Ah, so this is Stevie." Maddie moved further into the room and patted the cat on the head. He opened one eye then closed it again, purring lightly as he accepted her homage. "When did he move in?"

Jamie sat up so that Maddie could join her on the sofa. "Two weeks ago. He's settled in well."

"Good. That's excellent."

"So, what's up, Doc? Is this a social visit?"

"Afraid not." Now that she was here she wasn't sure how best to break the news. She plucked the envelope out of her pocket and held it out to her friend. "The results of your smear test came through today."

Jamie took it from her and held it with trembling fingers. "I guess it's not good news if you're delivering it personally." Her brown eyes were already welling up.

Maddie reached over and put a hand on her knee. "Look, it's a standard letter. It may not mean anything is terribly wrong. But you will have to undergo some more tests, just to make sure."

The envelope stayed unopened in Jamie's hands. "What does it say?"

Maddie kept her tone level, her patient-calming doctor's voice. "It just says the result was abnormal. This doesn't always mean anything dire. Minor changes in the cells in the cervix can throw up an abnormal result. Honestly, Jamie, another test will give a clearer indication of what's going on."

"Can you do this test?"

"No. I'm sorry; I'll have to refer you to the hospital. They have the proper equipment. But I can make sure you see a female gynaecologist."

The tears were flowing freely now. Stevie had jumped up onto Jamie's lap and was studying her face carefully.

"Jamie. This isn't life threatening. It happens a lot. Sometimes it might even mean the smear tests were mixed up. Or the changes in the cells might just be age-related. But I can't ignore it. I would be neglecting my duty of care if I didn't make sure you were checked out. The procedure's very simple. And it's better to know, don't you think? If there is a problem and it's caught at an early stage, it can be treated."

Maddie watched as Jamie slowly pulled herself together. She wiped her face on her sleeve. Stevie had moved onto the window ledge, still watchful.

"Sorry, I'm such a chicken shit. This year's been pretty hellish and this just tops it off."

"Hey, don't worry. I'm used to patients crying on me. Part of the job. Look, if you don't want to be on your own this evening, come over for tea. Even though Leo's not at home now, Laurel's still cooking for four."

"Okay, thanks. You sure Laurel won't mind."

"Not at all. I'll text her now. If you're ready to go I can give you a lift. My car's still at the Surgery.

"Right. Yeah, I'll just go to the loo."

†

Laurel set another place and cursed under her breath. Not that she objected in principle to having Jamie Steele at short notice, but she had hoped this would be the evening for just the three of them when she and Maddie could talk to Tay and find out what was going on with her. In the two weeks since Leo had been gone, there hadn't been a chance to sit down together.

She heard the front door open and straightened up. Time to go into hostess mode.

"Jamie, good to see you." The woman looked a bit peaky, she thought. Was this why Maddie had brought her home?

"I'm just going to get changed." Maddie was already on her way up the stairs. Laurel knew that the doctor would want to have a hot shower to wash away the stresses of the day along with the odours. It wasn't a job she could have coped with, having to see people with all their ailments and examine various body parts.

Laurel smiled at Jamie. "Come into the kitchen. You can open the wine."

Jamie followed her down the hallway and did as she was asked when Laurel handed her a bottle of red wine and an opener.

78

"We'll have that with dinner. Maddie usually likes a gin and tonic when she gets home. Would you like one?"

"Um. No thanks. I don't drink gin."

"Whiskey?"

"Yes, okay."

"With ice?"

"Sure. A couple of cubes, but no water."

Laurel looked in the cupboard. "There's a choice of Bushmills or Famous Grouse."

"Bushmills, please."

Laurel took the bottle out and a glass tumbler. She gave them to Jamie. "Pour what you want. The ice cubes are in the freezer."

She prepared a gin and tonic for Maddie and poured herself a glass of white wine. Luckily it was a simple meal tonight. The salad was already prepared. The lasagna was in the oven and the garlic bread didn't need to go in for another fifteen minutes. Time to enjoy a pre-dinner drink.

"Let's go and sit in the conservatory."

†

Laurel had been politely welcoming but Jamie had the feeling she wasn't particularly pleased to have her there. Her relationship with Laurel was always a bit stilted. Jamie had never completely got over the first impression of her as an ice queen.

The first swallow of Bushmills burned pleasantly down her throat. The shock of Maddie's news was wearing off. She was a grown up, after all. Everything the doctor had told her made sense. She would go and see a nice lady gynaecologist and undergo whatever tests were required. It didn't mean she was going to like it, and waiting for the result was going to be hell, but there really wasn't any other option. Another gulp of the fine Irish whiskey and she was starting to feel more positive about the whole thing.

Laurel was watching her, cold blue eyes seeming to bore into her. "Are you okay, Jamie?"

"Yes, fine thanks. Tough day at work, that's all." She wasn't going to share the last dodgy half hour of her life with Laurel and she knew Maddie had her Hippocratic oath to uphold.

"We haven't seen much of you the last few weeks."

And you haven't missed me, thought Jamie, but she knew what she was fishing for. No doubt Van had been on the phone. "I haven't been going out. Just getting Stevie settled in to his new surroundings."

"Oh? How did that happen?"

"I went over to Sasha's and she was happy to let me have him. Seems what's-her-name wasn't keen on having him there."

"Oh, well, that's nice."

Jamie looked at her over the rim of her glass. There were no furry creatures allowed in this house either. It had surprised her the first time she visited. They had enough garden space for at least a medium-size dog. And cats, to her mind, were really no bother. The Hope-Chambers children had lacked for nothing in their young lives, other than a pet or two.

Before she could think of something to say to Laurel's obvious disinterest in discussing Stevie's welfare, Maddie arrived in the room, hair still wet from her shower. She picked up her drink and sat down next to Jamie.

"Cheers," she said, lifting her glass. "Just what the doctor ordered."

Jamie smiled, but she suspected it was a line Laurel had heard many times before as her perfectly symmetrical face didn't crack.

"I'm thinking of buying a car," she said, to break the silence. "Thought I'd probably need one soon."

"Good idea," Maddie offered. "I was wondering how long you would keep up the cycling."

"I'll still cycle if the weather's not too bad. Rain's okay but I don't think I can handle ice and snow on these hills."

"What will you get?"

"Not sure. Any recommendations?"

"Depends how much you want to spend. But if we do have a cold winter, you'll want a four-wheel drive."

"Yeah, well, I was thinking of something I can throw the bike into, so it would have to at least be an estate car of some kind."

"Where will you park it? There's no street parking where you live."

"Well, that's the other big decision."

"No! Really. You're finally going to splash the cash and buy a house."

"Yeah. I've got to do something with the money. Stevie and I don't need much space, but I would like him to have somewhere he can be outside. He's been very good about being inside all the time, but I know he has cat dreams of exploring the wider world."

Laurel got up. "I'll just put the garlic bread in. Ready to eat in about fifteen."

"Thanks, love." Maddie watched her go into the kitchen before turning back to Jamie. "Have you checked anything out yet?"

"Sure. But the prices around here are outrageous. We're not even in footballers' wives' country."

"I know. But I wouldn't want to live anywhere else. Everything's so handy. And you can't beat the scenery."

Taylor burst in. "Hey, Mads, can I have a tenner?" She stopped in front of her mother before noticing Jamie. "Oops. Didn't know we had company. Hi Jamie."

"What do you need money for?" Maddie asked.

"Going to see a film."

"What happened to the ten pounds I gave you yesterday?"

The girl shifted from one foot to the other, looking down at the floor. "Don't know."

"Well, until you remember, you'll be staying in."

"But…"

"No, buts about it. I'm sure you've got some homework to do and I would like to check that before you go out again as well."

"Shit! I don't know why I live here." Taylor turned abruptly and stomped off.

Jamie bit her lip, trying not to laugh.

"That was out of order. I'll have to go and talk to her. You've got the right idea, Jamie. I'm sure a cat's a lot less trouble."

Left alone in the conservatory, Jamie finished her drink and stood up. She wandered over to the doorway to look out at the garden. It was the kind of place she would like for Stevie. Well away from the traffic on the main road and the railway line. But she couldn't afford a house this size. And she liked her small attic space. A compromise was needed. She would get her act together and start looking seriously at the weekend. It would help take her mind off the impending hospital visit.

✝

Sasha opened the front door and was assaulted by the unfamiliar smell of something cooking. She inhaled deeply. Something with garlic. Were they having company? It was a long time since Phoebe had done anything other than open a can of tuna in the kitchen.

A cookbook propped open on the counter, evidence of the chopping board having been used, and Phoebe bent over peering into the oven—all highly unusual sights.

"Who's coming for dinner?" she asked.

Phoebe straightened up and smiled at her sweetly. "No one, hon. Just us two."

"Um, right. What's the occasion?" Sasha didn't think she'd missed anything important. Phoebe's birthday was months away and they'd celebrated their first anniversary weeks ago.

"Nothing special. Just thought I would cook us a nice meal."

Sasha knew there was more to this than met the eye. The only appliances Phoebe was on intimate terms with on a regular basis were the toaster and the kettle.

"Great. Well, I'll go and get changed. How much time have I got?"

"Ten minutes. In the dining room."

If it had been a celebratory meal for a milestone event such as having reached number one in the Times bestseller list, they would have been going out to a restaurant. Acceptance of a manuscript and she would have been greeted with a glass of Champagne. But, actually cooking a meal? There was a hidden agenda. Perhaps Sasha was finally forgiven for her slight on the Septimus Seven book. But she hadn't yet come clean on where she had been the night she had tracked Jamie down. How could she admit to stalking her ex? The carefully cooked meal would be thrown in her face.

Downstairs again she found the seldom-used dining room table set for two with candles lit and soft music playing in the background. Red wine had been poured into the big globe-shaped glasses she knew they had but never used. Sasha checked the bottle. Not a name she recognised, but it looked expensive.

Phoebe came in with two small bowls and placed one in front of Sasha. "Garlic mushrooms. Your favourite." She sat down and raised her wine glass. "Here's to us, sweetie."

Sasha looked around. "Who are you? And what have you done with Phoebe?"

Her lover just gave her an enigmatic smile and sipped her wine. Sasha did the same. It was a very nice wine.

"Really, though, Feebs. What happened? You woke up today and decided to take up cooking? Not that I'm complaining, mind." She put a mushroom into her mouth. It was perfect. Just the right texture and flavouring. The garlic was there but not overpowering. "This is delicious. Have you been watching reruns of *MasterChef*?"

Another little smile. "Not at all. It's not that difficult, is it? I mean I can read and follow instructions." She reached over and placed a hand on Sasha's arm. "I just wanted to spoil you a little, Sash. And try to make up for being a bitch lately."

"Well, I'm sorry too. I shouldn't have said that about your book."

Phoebe shrugged. "Since you weren't going to do anything with it, I've sent it to Pearlman's. They're branching out into sci-fi now."

"Okay. Well, good luck with it." Sasha had gone to university with one of the Pearlman clan. She wasn't sure Phoebe would find much success there.

"So, I know you were fond of Stevie, but I've not missed the smell of the cat litter or his food. How did you hook up with her?"

There it was. Out in the open at last. But Sasha had prepared her statement and just needed to deliver it convincingly. "She phoned me at work. Said she was finding it hard on her own. I felt sorry for her. After all, she's got nothing and I've got you." She placed her hand over Phoebe's and gazed into her eyes. When Phoebe smiled back at her and didn't pull her hand away, Sasha knew she'd pulled it off. As long as her lover didn't find out about the sofa she was safe. And that wouldn't happen. They still had separate bank accounts. It had been another spur of the moment decision. She'd been appalled at Jamie's living conditions and knew it was her fault. The sofa was a sop to her conscience. Jamie had lost everything…lover, house, car, cat…and Sasha hadn't even been there for her when she lost her job. Not having a car wasn't a problem when she still lived in Bury and worked in Manchester with access to the frequent and reliable tram service. But now, working at some hick university miles from anywhere, Jamie was reduced to riding a bicycle to work.

†

She'd been stood up for a cat. So Laurel had informed her. Jamie was hiding out in her loft with Stevie. That had been her Saturday morning secret mission and she hadn't heard from her since. Was it even worth pursuing what seemed more and more like a lost cause? The problem was that every time Van closed her eyes she was visualising the damn woman—in the ass-hugging lycra, following her up the stairs to her room, playing a game on her Xbox, their hands and knees touching, and Jamie laughing. Van just couldn't get Jamie out of her head.

"Come on, Van. You're forty-five, not a fucking teenager. She's obviously not interested. Get over it."

"Talking to yourself. First signs of dementia." Connor had popped his head over the screen and was scrutinising her.

"Take a hike, boy."

Instead of taking the hint, he scooted around the screen on his chair. "Is she really that hot?" he whispered.

"Who?"

"This woman you're obsessing over."

"I'm not obsessing over anyone."

"So why have you had your head up your butt for the last two weeks?"

Van looked at him, but couldn't muster up her usual scary stare that would send him scurrying back to his desk.

"You wouldn't understand."

"Try me."

"What do you know about unrequited love? You wouldn't even be able to spell it."

"Oh, I know plenty. About that." His ears reddened as he spoke, and he had found a spot on the floor by his feet that was fascinating.

"I thought you were seeing that girl from Accounts. You two seem pretty tight."

"She's just a mate."

"So, what gives?" She could sense his unease.

"I'm like you," he mumbled.

"What, a sad old dyke?"

"You know what I mean." He was still staring at the spot on the floor.

She took pity on him and patted his knee. "Look, we can't talk about this here. Let's see if we can get a break together later on. Lou will cover for us."

He nodded to the floor and sidled back to his desk, shoulders hunched.

Van looked up at her screen, relieved to see an incoming call.

†

Van couldn't believe she'd offered to do this. But once Connor had confided in her and told her his problem, she'd been unable to say no. The last time she'd been in a club, the hit song was Sophie Ellis-Bextor's "Murder on the Dancefloor," and that had to be at least ten years ago. Van didn't know any of the current numbers and her dance skills had never been great. A slow number she could manage, letting her partner lead, so she just had to move her feet vaguely in time to the music.

Connor handed her a bottle of Corona and grinned at her. "This is great. I think that guy over there's checking me

87

out," he shouted in her ear, waving his bottle back towards the bar.

"Looks like you're set for the night. Don't worry about me." Van leant back against the wall and sucked on the bottle, hoping she was managing to look cool or whatever the word was now, not some ageing fag-hag titillated by the sight of so many fit, heaving bodies.

"So, what do I do?"

"Connor, we talked about this. Let him know you're interested. You can't expect him to be a fucking mind reader."

He looked panicked again. All the way up Princess Street he'd been a bag of nerves, asking her if he looked all right, anxious that he wouldn't be out of place. She'd reassured him he would be fine. In fact, she'd been surprised he scrubbed up so well. The tight white t-shirt showed off his pecs to advantage. His office wear consisted of loose white shirts and black trousers that wouldn't have looked out of place as a school uniform for the class nerd. The hip-hugging jeans he was wearing tonight didn't leave anything to the imagination. She didn't think he'd have any problem making a favourable impression.

"Look," she'd told him, "You don't have to cop off with anyone tonight. Unless you want to, of course. Just have a few drinks, dance, have a good time."

They'd spent ten minutes outside the club as he had another panic attack. She'd finally told him to stop being a chicken-shit, she wasn't going to stay outside any longer freezing her bits off.

Now it looked like she was left playing gooseberry. The few women she could see were young enough to be her daughters. A responsible parent wouldn't have let any of them out of the house dressed as they were. Not to mention the amount of hardware adorning their faces. Then she spotted someone who looked as out of place as she did. It took her a moment to think where she'd seen her before. Jamie's ex. What was her name? Sara? Sheila? Something starting with "S." Stevie? No, that was the cat's name. Sasha, that was it. She remembered thinking it was a good name for a pet. What was she doing here? It didn't look like her scene, either.

Watching the few women gyrating on the dance floor she wondered what it would be like to dance with Jamie. Maybe with her she would be able to lose her self-consciousness and simply enjoy the sensation of being held by those strong arms as the music wove a magical force field around them. She shook her head. A fantasy that wasn't likely to come true, much as she wanted it to. Was there anything sadder than a forty-five year old wallflower? She'd stick it out for another half hour, then Connor was on his own.

†

The club scene had certainly changed since the last time Sasha had been a regular. Most of the patrons looked too young to be out on a school night. The flashing lights on the dance floor were making it hard to see faces clearly, but she saw a woman leaning against the wall who looked vaguely familiar, probably the mother of one of these spotty youths. Glancing away her target came into view. He was talking to a younger man but they didn't look like they were intimate. She pushed her way through the crowd around the bar and touched his arm to get his attention.

It took him a moment to place her. But, of course, it had to be several years since they'd last met. A book fair, probably Frankfurt.

"Sasha! Hey, long time no see."

"Phil."

Even dressed as he was in trendy leather trousers and matching vest, he was still far too old for this crowd. But she would give him points for trying. It wouldn't be long before he was shaving his head to minimise the fact that he was going bald.

"Need to talk." Her words got carried off into the swirl of lights.

He understood though and nodded. After a quick few words to his companion, he indicated that she should follow him.

Once outside again, the streets heaving with more bodies, some looking for action, some on a sightseeing tour—he led her down a side street and into a downstairs café she wouldn't have known existed. It looked like a 1950s American diner with faux leather bench seats in booths lined up along one wall, and was blessedly quiet, just one couple holding hands and whispering to each other at the far end. They sat down in a booth near the door.

"Would you like something to drink," Phil asked.

"Do they do ice cream floats?"

Phil raised an eyebrow.

"Sorry, I'm expecting the Fonz to appear any minute. A black coffee would be great."

Phil waved to the person who had arrived behind the counter. Moments later two mugs appeared in front of them.

Philip Pearlman carefully stirred a small amount of sugar in his. "It tastes better than it looks," he said, seeing

Sasha's hesitation. "So, what brings you out to the gay side of town."

"I think you have an idea. Have you actually read the thing?"

"I've read enough to think it has promise."

"You're not just leading her on?"

"Look, Sash, your girlfriend's old enough to make her own decisions. You've rejected her manuscript, so she's come to me. What's the problem?"

"I don't want to see her get hurt."

"Bit late for that. Rejection cuts deep for any writer. Anyway, I'm just having a chat with her Monday. If she's amenable to my input, I think we'll enjoy a fruitful working relationship. Don't blame me if *The Moons of Septimus Seven* turns out to be the new *Game of Thrones*. You had your chance."

Sasha sipped her coffee which was surprisingly good. She'd expected something the flavour of burnt excrement from the first impressions of the place.

"I hope you're not planning on telling Phoebe that."

"Why not? She's taken a brave step venturing into a new genre. So, okay, she wants to publish under another pen name. That's understandable. If it turns out to be a flop, Felix LeMar disappears into the black hole from whence he came."

"You don't back flops. So why now?"

Again that smile, the one that always made her want to punch him. "Why not? Deal with it Sasha. It's not my problem." He stood up and adjusted his trousers, an unendearing habit she remembered from their uni days when he had taken every opportunity to remind her what she didn't have. "Gotta run. At least I have a chance of getting laid tonight." He gave her that sly smile again, and a small wave as he walked out the door and ran back up the steps.

"Fuck you," she said to the empty seat, realising that he'd also left her to pay for the coffees.

Chapter Five

Phoebe looked up at the building and was impressed. This was more like it. SRP's offices were out in the boonies, but this imposing red brick structure just off Dean Street was the business. Pearlman's would be a step up if she could get a foot in the door. Phoebe walked through the glass doors into a foyer that had retained all the features of its art deco past. The receptionist asked her to sign in, gave her a badge, and told her to take the stairs up to the next floor. She suspected there was a lift hidden somewhere for dignitaries and deliveries, but she didn't qualify. Still, it was an experience just walking up the wide staircase, her hand brushing the sleek wooden bannister.

At the top she was met by a man sporting the Steve Jobs look of black polo shirt and jeans. He had a lot of teeth and not much hair, but at least his smile looked genuinely welcoming.

"Phoebe, pleased to meet you. Philip Pearlman. Do come in." He ushered her into a large, high-ceilinged room that, despite its size, had the look of being in someone's home. There was a desk with a computer on it shoved in a corner. The main focus was the arrangement of sofas and chairs in front of a fireplace with what looked like the original ceramic tiles on the surround. And real coals in the grate.

He followed her gaze and said, "Yes, it is a real fire. Smokeless fuel though. Please, have a seat."

She sat down at one end of the sofa near the fireplace. The tray on the table in front of her contained more items that looked like they had come out of a museum. *Was that a teapot shaped like an old motorcar? And the handle of that jug looked like a golfer.* Again, Philip Pearlman seemed to divine her thoughts. "Not original Clarice Cliff's I'm afraid. Just some pieces I've picked up here and there at auctions. Tea?"

"Yes, please. Milk no sugar." Phoebe sat back and took in the rest of the room. Two walls were lined with books. The floor-to-ceiling windows either side of the fireplace looked like they had the original frames. Well, they would be, she thought. This had to be a listed building. No UPVC double glazing allowed here, even if it did mean putting up with hearing the traffic on the street below, and blasts of cold air on windy days coming through the cracks.

Once the tea was poured, Philip got down to business. "Thanks for coming in Phoebe. I'm a big fan of your Felicity Lemon books. Just wondering why you've ventured into Science Fiction?"

"It's something I've dabbled in over the years. I've had this story kicking around for some time and wanted to see if it would fly, so to speak."

"Well, it certainly has wings. But at this stage, I'm not sure it will get off the ground." He patted the pages of her manuscript which she noticed now was lying on the table next to the tea tray.

Phoebe sipped her tea to give herself the chance to swallow and not say something she might regret. She put the cup and saucer back on the table.

"Is that a polite rejection?"

"Not at all. I wouldn't have invited you here to say something that could have been said in an email. Obviously, if you were a new writer, we wouldn't be having this conversation. But I know and admire your work. I have read through the manuscript. Again, I wouldn't have done that for an unknown."

"I still get the feeling you're telling me it's rubbish."

"No. What I'm leading up to saying is that I think, with just a bit more work, I would be happy to recommend it to a publisher. However, there were a few gaps in the story that need filling out."

Phoebe sat back, relieved. She smiled at him. "Okay. That sounds encouraging."

"It's more than encouraging, Phoebe." He steepled his hands together in a way that reminded her of the careers guidance counsellor at school. "You can bring this to life with just a few tweaks here and there. I get what you're doing with the dragons and the music and the stone circles. You've got a blend of myth and magic along with spaceships and mysterious planets. All the classic elements of fantasy and science fiction. But I would like to see you concentrate more on the mythical elements with the personifications of Morgana and the Merlin."

He picked up the manuscript and flipped through to a page marked with a pink post-it note. "For example, this passage here where Merlin and Alethea are travelling by boat across the drowned Vale of the White Horse."

Phoebe listened, entranced, as he read her words back to her.

"'For a time,' the Merlin said, 'I travelled those roads, stopped at that inn. My land, the one I would call my homeland, lies further west. At least, it was west when north was south and south was north. Now it is east of here. But nothing is ever final. I am from the sunken lands, you are from the stars. Together we journey through the mists of time to discover another beginning.'"

He put the pages down and gave her a searching look. "Your words have power, Phoebe. Power that you can harness with the imagery of dancing giants and circles of light. I believe you can do this. It will be a work to be proud of. Think big. Think *Game of Thrones*, *Lord of the Rings*, *Harry* fucking *Potter*, even. Bring it to life for me, Phoebe."

When she walked out of the building half an hour later, she was floating. A celebratory drink in her favourite wine bar was in order and then she would make plans for the research Philip had advised her to undertake.

Walking down the street, smiling at all the passersby, Phoebe knew that a glass or two of wine, or even a cocktail, wasn't going to be enough. She wanted to share this joy with someone. Sasha was at work and probably fantasising about her imaginary life with Jamie Steele. Phoebe thumbed through the contact list on her phone and stopped at a name. Perfect. She texted: *Meet me Radisson half an hour*. The reply pinged back almost immediately, as she knew it would. A simple *K* in response. A woman of few words, but she liked her that way. Sasha was such hard work these days, she was beginning to wonder if it was worth the effort.

✝

The colposcopy hadn't been as bad as Jamie had anticipated. Maddie explained the procedure to her before she went to the hospital. And the fact that she would be in and out in a day had eased her worries as well. She hadn't wanted to impose on Maddie to look after Stevie while she was gone.

Now she just had to wait for the results. That was the really hard part. Although Maddie had assured her that if there was anything seriously wrong she would be called back for further treatment very quickly.

Waiting outside the classroom for the lecturer to finish up, Jamie hoped it would be a quiet week. She'd spent some time over the weekend checking out car dealerships and real estate agents online. There were two house possibilities she wanted to look at so she was going to have a busy Saturday. She had arranged to see both houses in the morning. If the used Seat Alhambra she was going to check out that evening was as good as it looked on the website, she'd probably be able to pick it up on Saturday as well. It was reasonably priced for an MPV and she needed that size of vehicle for the bike. A smaller car with a bike rack was an option, but she didn't like the racks. And, as Maddie had said, she would appreciate the larger vehicle if they had a winter of ice and snow.

The droning voice had stopped and Jamie risked a glance through the window. The lecturer saw her and waved her in. She hated having to go into classrooms full of students, but there were only six in this group. A quick in and out to replace the batteries on the whiteboard remote, and she was on her way back to the sanctuary of the IT Services office.

Mike wasn't there, but Jonathan was; a rare appearance these days. He had been "working from home" a lot, although what he did from home was a mystery to her and Mike.

"Hi Jonathan. I'm glad you're here."

"Oh, really. You've missed me. I'm touched."

"Don't get too excited. No, I just wanted to know how I get a car park permit. I've heard they're like gold dust."

"Not surprised you're giving up the bike. I'm amazed you've lasted this long."

Jamie reset the coffee machine and looked over at him. "So, what do I have to do?"

"No sweat. I'll talk to Admin. Shouldn't be a problem. When do you need it by?"

"I'm going to look at a car tonight and, hopefully, I'll be driving in next Monday."

"Okay, leave it with me. And let me know as soon as you have a registration number."

He looked tired, she thought, and it was only ten o'clock. "Do you want a coffee?"

"No thanks. I'm not staying long today."

She wanted to ask him what was going on, but something stopped her. He would tell them if he wanted them to know.

After he'd left the office, she sat back and looked at her screensaver. Stevie's green eyes stared back at her. She smiled at his image and wished he could talk. Her list of people she could talk to could be counted on one hand, minus the thumb. Her parents didn't count. Since their separation her mother hadn't wanted any contact with her. She had never approved of her daughter's "lifestyle" and once Josh was gone, any maternal feelings she might have had died with her son. Her dad had moved to Spain and was living with a woman twenty years his junior. They exchanged emails and Skyped a few times a year, but he was immersed in his new life. They each voiced vague promises to visit when they spoke, but she knew it wasn't likely to happen unless she made the effort.

There was one person she should talk to. She felt guilty about not contacting her before. Getting Stevie settled in, the hospital visit preying on her mind, the weeks had passed and now she wondered if she'd left it too long. After all, Van was an attractive woman and probably had other options. But Jamie had enjoyed the few times they'd spent together. It was worth a try. She could only say no.

Jamie pulled her phone out of her pocket and sent a text to Van.

†

Van punched the air and sat back smiling inanely. Jamie had texted her and wanted to meet up again. Result!

"Have you been taking happy pills?" Connor propped his chin on the top of the divider screen and gave her a goofy smile. He'd been smiling a lot lately.

"No need. I've got another date."

"You're so sad, you know that?"

"No sadder than you, lover boy."

99

His computer pinged and his head disappeared. She was grateful she wasn't going to have to hear about his latest conquest. One visit to a gay club and he thought he was stud of the month.

Van started thinking about what she was going to wear. Jamie had suggested meeting at a restaurant near Victoria station, so she really didn't have to dress up unless she was dressing to impress. It would be nice to think Jamie wanted more than just a dinner date but she had the feeling she was going to have to move slowly on this one. Any sudden movements and Jamie would be on the run.

She managed to avoid talking to Connor until the afternoon break when he followed her outside. Listening to him enthuse about the club and the opportunities it presented for his burgeoning sex life, she was reminded of her younger self and let him prattle on. Her thoughts were elsewhere, thinking about how she could draw Jamie out without scaring her off.

The wet weather meant that her choice of clothing was easily decided. She opted for casual, not flashy. The restaurant was only a tram ride away, and she was able to make it inside the door without getting too blown about by the wind and rain. She spotted Jamie right away, seated by the window, a bottle of red wine already on the table.

Jamie stood up when she came over and offered to take her coat. Van smiled and let her take charge.

"I've already ordered wine. Hope that's okay with you."

The sound of that voice, the one she'd been hearing in her head for the last few weeks, she was only able to nod and watch as Jamie poured a generous measure into her glass. What on earth could her ex have been thinking?

Looking at Jamie's long fingers as they picked up her glass, Van thought she might not last the evening without wanting to make a move on this woman. Her earlier resolve to take it slow was melting as she felt captivated by her companion's every movement.

They ordered their food and, while they were waiting for their starters, Van told Jamie about the trip to the club on Canal Street, how Connor had been as nervous as a kid being taken to his first day at school. But after seeing him through the school gates, so to speak, she hadn't been needed anymore. She left out the significant detail of having seen Sasha there.

Jamie opened up a bit as they ate, telling her about buying a car and plans for serious house hunting at the weekend. Van felt better knowing that Jamie had been busy getting her life sorted out, that she hadn't just been ignoring her. But she had her doubts that anything other than a friendship was developing between them. Either Van's flirting skills were sadly lacking or Jamie just wasn't ready to pick up on the obvious signals she was putting out.

✝

As the train pulled out of Victoria Station, Jamie realised she had enjoyed herself during the meal. It had been fun to see Van again and laugh. When did the laughter stop with her and Sasha? Was that when their relationship began to die? Jamie was starting to think maybe Sasha had done her a favour by leaving the way she did. The distress she'd been harbouring for the last year was starting to fade. From the looks Van had been giving her while they ate, it was clear she was interested in something more than the occasional dinner date. Maybe it was time she moved on. Having Stevie back had helped, and her sleep was no longer disturbed with waking to the acute sense of betrayal and hurt that had dominated every aspect of her life for the past year.

Whatever the results of the colposcopy, Jamie was feeling more in control of things now. The car she looked at Monday evening was just right and the price was right too. The Alhambra had already gone so she got the next model down, a Leon. It was a smaller, sleeker looking car, and still had space for the bike once the back seats were folded down. And, not that she would buy a car simply because she liked the colour, but she was pleased that it was a smart-looking aqua blue, and not the drab grey—named "silver" in all the brochures—that seemed to be the colour of every other car on the road. Best of all, it would be ready for her to collect on Saturday.

Walking back through the town from the train station, she savoured the freshness of the late evening air, a light breeze ruffling her hair. It hadn't been too cold yet, but there was the promise of early morning frosts to come. Although she loved cycling to work, she knew she would appreciate having the car in the coming months. And after some gentle persuasion from her Search and Rescue buddy, Andy, she had decided to join one of the local cycling clubs. They did regular fifty-mile rides on Saturdays or Sundays, and in the good weather, Wednesday evenings as well.

A gang of kids passed her, shouting and shoving at each other. She stayed out of their way and moved on slowly once they'd disappeared round the corner. The sound of someone retching nearby caught her attention. The figure crouched on the pavement looked familiar.

"Taylor?"

The girl heaved again, a thin stream of bile trailing out of her mouth. Jamie crouched down next to her. She put a hand on her shoulder.

"Hey. It's me, Jamie. You'll be okay. Just try and breathe."

After a few breaths and no more heaves, Jamie gently brought the youngster to her feet.

"Come on. It's not far to my place. Let's get you cleaned up."

Moving slowly, they made their way up to Jamie's room. She rinsed out one of her two wine glasses in the bathroom sink and filled it with water from a litre bottle next to the bike.

After she'd drunk it, Taylor moaned. "I can't go home like this."

"Well, why don't you have a shower? I'll find something for you to change into."

Stevie had woken up when they came in and he joined Jamie on the sofa while they waited for Taylor to finish her shower. She stroked behind his ears and met his green-eyed gaze. "It's not what you think, buddy. She's only sixteen and she needs our help." He settled down on her lap and let out a contented sigh as he closed his eyes again.

Taylor looked a bit better when she emerged from behind the screen wearing the sweatshirt and shorts that Jamie had left out for her. The sweatshirt, which was loose on Jamie, was a tight fit on the teenager. Her wet hair draped lankly around her shoulders.

Disturbing Stevie by standing up, Jamie indicated the sofa for Taylor to sit on and fetched her another glass of water.

"You probably shouldn't eat anything for a while, but you need to re-hydrate."

Stevie glanced between Jamie and Taylor as if weighing up his options for getting the most comfortable position.

Jamie waited a few more minutes before asking the obvious questions. "How did you get into this state? And where are your friends?"

"Don't know. I don't remember much."

"So, they just left you puking your guts up in the street. Some friends."

"Yeah, well…"

"Are your parents expecting you home?"

"No. I'm supposed to be staying with Annie."

The girl looked utterly miserable.

Jamie noticed the red mark on her cheek. "What happened? Did you get into a fight?"

"Sort of," Taylor couldn't meet her eyes.

"Look, I'm only trying to help. If you don't want to talk to me, fine. But I think you should talk to someone."

Stevie had decided to curl up in the chair and the sound of him snorting softly in his sleep was all that could be heard in the room for the next few minutes. Jamie waited patiently.

"Told Shaz I love her," Taylor mumbled eventually.

"And Shaz is…?"

"Just this girl in my year. I thought she liked me. She hates me now. They all hate me."

"How long have you had…feelings, for Shaz?"

"Since, like forever."

"How long's that?" Jamie knew that forever, in terms of a love-struck teenager, probably wasn't very long at all.

"Since she moved here, last term."

"Shaz. Is that her real name?"

"No. It's Shannon."

"Have you kissed her?"

"I tried to but she shoved me away."

"Haven't you talked to your parents about this?"

"Mum hates me because I'm not like Leo, and Mads is always too busy."

"What about when she takes you snowboarding? Couldn't you talk to her then? When it's just the two of you."

"It doesn't seem right. I don't want to spoil our day out."

"Why would it spoil anything? Maddie loves you. Laurel does too, but maybe she's not good at showing it."

A loud burst of music startled them and Stevie glared at the two humans accusingly. Taylor got up and pulled her phone out of her bag.

"Oh, shit. The bastards!"

"What is it?"

Taylor handed her the phone and sat down, hanging her head between her knees.

Jamie looked at the picture of Taylor as she had found her, puking up on the pavement. The picture disappeared after a few seconds. "Oh, it's Snapchat, isn't it? So that's not too bad. At least it's not on Facebook."

"Wouldn't matter if it was on Facebook. That's for sharing baby photos with granny. I'll bet someone filmed me. It'll be on YouTube as well." A blaring horn startled them both. Leo's face appeared on the screen of Taylor's phone. She let the annoying sound continue.

"You better answer it. If he's seen the picture, he'll be worried."

Taylor accepted the call and held the phone to her ear. "Yeah, I'm okay. Thanks. Look, don't tell Mum, please."

Jamie could hear him asking where she was.

"I'm at Jamie's. You know, Mads' friend. Rides a bike." She looked close to tears again. "No, Leo, don't. I'm okay here." She stood up and dropped the phone onto the sofa. "Fucking prick. He's phoning Mum. And, guess what? He saw it on YouTube. I'm in so much shit now. Mum's going to kill me."

Jamie stood as well. Tears were leaking out of Taylor's eyes and she was starting to shake. "Hey, come on. Your parents love you. They'll want to know you're okay. Calm down." Without thinking about it, Jamie stepped in and held the weeping girl close.

†

Maddie was negotiating the narrow lane carefully.

"Can't you go any faster?" Laurel gripped the sides of the seat.

"Not if we want to get there in one piece."

"What's she doing at Jamie's anyway? What's the woman thinking? She better not have touched her."

"Fuck's sake, Laurel. As far as I can tell, Jamie's helped her out. Calm down."

The doctor stopped the car on the double yellow lines outside the house and Laurel leapt out before Maddie had time to pull the handbrake up and switch the headlights off. But she couldn't get inside until Maddie arrived at the front door and put the code in.

Laurel raced up the stairs, her heart pounding. At least her regular Keep Fit regime paid off as she reached the top without having to stop for breath. She opened the door to the loft and her worst fears were confirmed. Jamie was holding her daughter in a close embrace. She launched in without thinking.

"Get off her, you pervert!" she screamed and started pulling Jamie away.

"Mum, no!"

Laurel felt a tearing on her trouser leg. She lashed out with her foot but the creature had latched on with its claws.

"Get it off me," she shouted. She kicked back again and the cat flew half way across the floor towards the sofa.

†

Maddie arrived in the room in time to see Laurel's foot connect with Stevie and witnessed the initial shock on Jamie's face turn swiftly to anger. Laurel's leg was bleeding from a long scratch but it didn't look too deep. She could deal with that later. Taylor was looking as upset as Jamie. Time to get her out of here and ask questions later.

"Laurel, take Tay down to the car." She handed the keys over.

Jamie had gone over to the cat and was making soothing noises.

"What happened?" Maddie asked, keeping her voice level.

"I found her in the street. She's had a shower. Her clothes are in that bin bag." Jamie now had Stevie in her arms and didn't look up as she spoke.

Maddie glanced around and saw the black bag next to the bike by the wall. "Right. Well, better get her home. Thanks."

Jamie didn't move, just stayed where she was, stroking the cat's black fur.

There wasn't any more Maddie could say so she picked up the bag and left.

The drive home didn't take long but the tension inside the vehicle was palpable. Taylor was sobbing quietly in the back seat. Laurel had joined her there, but Tay moved away from her and huddled against the far door. In the rearview mirror, Maddie could see the thin-set line of Laurel's lips. So much for the night of passion she'd had planned when Tay said she was staying over at her friend's tonight.

Inside the house, she told Laurel to put the kettle on.

"I'm not sitting around drinking cups of tea. I want to know what's been going on."

"Plenty of time for that. I need to treat that scratch on your leg. Tay, why don't you go and get warm in bed? I'll come up in a bit."

Taylor had already started up the stairs without a backward glance to either of them.

Laurel stomped off down the hallway. Maddie sighed and fetched her medical bag out of the hall closet.

Her wife was pouring a large glass of brandy when she arrived in the kitchen, anger still pouring off her in waves.

"Come on, love. Sit down. I need to clean this up before it gets infected."

"If it does, I'm suing the bitch. And that animal needs to be put down as well."

"You were attacking Jamie. That cat behaves more like a dog. He's obviously devoted to her. And I think it's likely we owe Jamie an apology."

"What? She was seducing our baby."

"I don't think so." Maddie carefully swabbed Laurel's leg with disinfectant. As she'd thought, the scratch wasn't deep and was easily covered with a small plaster. "I'm going to see if Tay will talk to me. Perhaps you should call Leo and see what he knows. All he said before was that she was in trouble."

Tay was curled up in bed with the duvet wrapped securely around her body. Maddie could just see the top of her nose. She sat down on the edge and put a hand on the bundle.

"Talk to me, sweetheart. I can't help you if I don't know what's wrong."

"Everything's wrong."

Maddie stroked the duvet. She needed to get her daughter to talk. Whatever she thought was wrong, it didn't have to be life threatening. Yet teenagers killed themselves for less.

"Whatever it is, you just need to remember we all love you."

"Mum shouldn't have kicked Stevie."

"No, she shouldn't. I'll go and see Jamie tomorrow and apologise." She pulled the bottle of tablets out of her pocket and shook one out into her hand. "Come on, Taser, sit up and take this. It'll help you sleep."

The use of her old nickname made Tay look at her. She snaked a hand out from under the cover and took the pill, popping it into her mouth quickly. Maddie passed her the glass and she sat up just enough to be able to swallow a mouthful, before lying back down.

Maddie watched as her eyes closed and in a few minutes the even breathing told her the girl was asleep. Now it was just the small matter of placating her wife.

✝

The day at work had never seemed so long. Jamie hadn't wanted to leave Stevie alone when she left in the morning. He seemed okay but she was sure he'd been traumatised. She had gone over to the supermarket at lunchtime and bought him some treats.

She had just settled down with a glass of wine, Stevie purring contentedly on her lap when there was a tentative knock on the door.

"Sorry, bud," she said softly, "Looks like we've got company."

There was another knock, a bit firmer this time.

"Come in," she called.

Maddie appeared in the doorway. "Hi. Sorry to disturb you."

"You on your own?"

"Yes."

"Okay. Well, would you like some wine?"

"Sure."

"Help yourself. The bottle's on the bookcase."

Maddie poured a small measure for herself, glancing around for the best place to sit before perching on the other end of the sofa.

"I wanted to apologise for yesterday. Laurel was out of order. Is he okay?"

Jamie looked down at Stevie who had closed his eyes again when Maddie sat down. "Yeah, looks like it. Has Tay told you what happened?"

"She just said she fell out with her friends and she'd had too much to drink."

"That's it?"

"Yes. And I know what you're thinking. There has to be more to it than that. But I don't want to push her. We're keeping her off from school for the rest of the week."

"What about the online stuff?"

"Luckily Leo was able to find out who posted the video. Laurel spoke to the boy's mother and he's removed it but it had already been seen by a lot of people."

"Yeah, I'll bet. Oh, Tay left her phone here. I switched it off because there were loads of texts coming through. It's..."

"On the bookcase?"

They looked at each other and laughed, easing the tension.

"Thanks for looking after her, Jamie. I hate to think what would have happened if you hadn't found her. Laurel wants to make it up to you for lashing out last night. She asked me to invite you over for dinner."

"Right." Jamie didn't think she could sit across from Laurel making polite conversation just yet. Maddie was watching her closely, waiting for an answer. Best to let her friend down gently. "Maybe not this week. I've got a lot on." She told Maddie about the car and the house viewings.

"That's great." Maddie gulped down her wine. "Better go. I promised I'd be home early tonight."

"Don't forget the phone."

The doctor picked it up off the bookcase. "She's been wanting a new one for a while. I was going to wait until Christmas, but now seems like a good time."

Jamie grimaced. "I saw a few of the texts before I switched it off. I don't think she'll want to see them."

"Hmm. I might just tell her it broke in the scuffle last night. Thanks again, Jamie. I don't know how we can ever repay you."

"Well, there is one thing you could do?"

"What's that?"

"See if you can speed up my results."

Maddie smiled. "Yes. I'll see what I can do. Catch you later."

She closed the door carefully behind her, and Jamie listened to her steps recede and the front door opening and closing.

"Well, that's that, buddy. Guess I better see about our dinner. I'm thinking fish and chips. We both deserve a treat."

†

Phoebe had been acting strangely all week. Ever since her Monday morning meeting with Philip Pearlman. Sasha wondered what the little shit had promised her and just hoped he hadn't raised her expectations unrealistically. *Game of Thrones, my arse!* She was sure he was only doing it to spite her.

Still, maybe she owed him one. After the romantic dinner with Phoebe, Sasha experienced a return to the early days of their relationship when they couldn't get enough of each other. Phoebe's ardour had been particularly intense on the Monday evening after her meeting with Phil. She had pounced on Sasha the moment she got in the door and initiated a sexual encounter that started in the hallway before Sasha had taken her coat off. They only made it as far as the living room before they were both naked and beyond caring about the discomfort of lying on a cold hardwood floor. When Phoebe turned on the charm, she was impossible to resist.

Later, when they had finally made it upstairs to the more comfortable surroundings of their bedroom, and were lying sated in each other's arms, Sasha had ventured to ask, "Why do you want to write fantasy or sci-fi, or whatever it is?"

"I'm fed up with a life of crime. It's so limiting. Sci-fi opens up whole new worlds to be explored."

"But your crime series is successful."

"Oh, come on, Sash. You know it's just ticking along. I'm doing okay, but I'm not hitting the heights, am I? No one's going to remember me as a rival to P.D. James or Ruth Rendell. No one's ever referred to me as the 'Queen of Crime'."

"But it's quite a leap, from murder to stargazing."

Phoebe moved out of her embrace. "All right. I get it. You don't think I can do this. You've made it clear you think the book is rubbish."

"I didn't really mean that. It's just not my thing. I'm sorry."

"Yeah. Well at least Philip believes in me."

Sasha sighed. "You know we used to call him PeePee at school."

"Yes, he told me you were perfectly horrid. A right little bully."

"That's not true. He was just as forthcoming with insults when he could find someone to hide behind."

"Anyway, I'm doing this Sasha, whether you like it not."

Another statement of intent, another ultimatum, but at least Phoebe was speaking to her now.

†

Laurel sounded distraught on the phone. Van had no experience with kids but she'd always admired the way her friend had eased into motherhood. With the long hours her partner worked, most of the day-to-day parenting fell on Laurel. She was the one who had to make the tough decisions, and then Maddie was able to turn up and smooth things over. Laurel's feeling that she was failing with Taylor had been growing ever since the girl hit puberty.

"I didn't mean to lash out at the damn cat, Van. But it scratched me. Now both Mads and Tay think I'm some kind of monster."

"Is Stevie all right?" Van knew that this would be what hurt Jamie most. Their date the night before had ended too early as far as she was concerned. Jamie hadn't wanted to miss the last train back to Hebden Bridge because of Stevie. And then she'd got caught up in this family drama.

"Yes. Maddie's been round to apologise. I asked her to invite Jamie over for dinner but she said she's too busy this week. So it looks like I've screwed up that friendship as well."

"Maybe she really is busy." Van hoped that was the case. So far her texts to Jamie had gone unanswered. "She told me she's getting a car and going house hunting at the weekend."

"She told us that weeks ago. So, she's actually doing it?"

"Yes. She's lined up a couple of viewings for Saturday."

"Okay. Well, if you're talking to her, please let her know I'm sorry about jumping to conclusions and kicking the cat."

"Will do."

After she ended the call, Van wondered if Jamie was still upset by the incident. Maybe that's why she wasn't answering her messages. What if Stevie was hurt and she'd had to take him to the vet? She hadn't met the cat in person yet, but she knew what he meant to Jamie. *Damn you, Laurel,* she thought. *You better not have messed up my chance of getting anywhere with this one.* The few times they had spent together she had felt there was something growing between them. Jamie had just given her the briefest of hugs before setting off to catch her train after their dinner together. The feeling of their bodies touching had sent shivers down her spine. Maybe Connor was right. She was obsessing over this woman. She'd thought she was too old to be having wet dreams but now she was waking up in the night, touching herself and finding she was dripping and needing to bring herself to an unsatisfactory but necessary climax before being able to fall back into a troubled sleep.

She wanted to see Jamie again but she didn't know how to do it without letting her desperation show. Jamie had been badly hurt by her ex and it was understandable that she wasn't going to rush into anything. Still, she had to do something to move things on. As a Geordie friend was fond of saying, "shy bairns get nowt." Time to act.

†

Things were working out. Jamie could feel it. The car was ready for collection on Friday evening, which made things easier for Saturday. She didn't have to rush the house viewings. It would have been a bit mad, having to bike back to Huddersfield to get the car. And Jonathan had been easy about her taking off an hour earlier so she would miss some of the traffic build up on the bypass.

After she'd completed the paperwork and shaken hands with the salesman, Jamie loaded the bike into the boot, removing the front wheel first. It fit perfectly. She sat behind the steering wheel for a few minutes to familiarise herself with the controls. Even though it was a used car, it still had a new car smell. Obviously it had been cleaned thoroughly, but she was pleased there was no lingering odour of smoke or wet dog.

Driving out of the town was a new experience, a different perspective from her usual perch on the saddle of the bike. She took a longer route that meant she could avoid the bypass and give herself time to get the feel of the car.

Earlier that week she had scoped out a quiet street near her building where she could park. One of the few streets that wasn't metered or designated parking for residents only. She removed the bike, popped the wheel back in place and cycled slowly around the corner envisaging a quiet night in with Stevie. She would introduce him to the car in the morning.

116

It was just getting dark as she walked up the steps to the front door of the house.

"Hey, don't hit me!" a voice called out.

Startled, Jamie almost dropped the bike before realising it was Van huddled by the doorway.

"Did we have a date?"

"No. But Laurel told me what happened the other night. I wanted to see how you were."

"Okay. Well, I…" Jamie was at a loss for words.

"Look, I don't need to stay. She was worried about you…and Stevie."

"Why? Because I didn't want to go round for dinner? And I don't think she's at all concerned about Stevie's welfare."

"I'm sorry. Obviously this wasn't a good idea." Van started to move away.

"No. It's okay. Come on up. I just need to have a shower."

Van followed her up the stairs and Jamie was glad there was still some wine left from Maddie's visit the night before. She poured a glass for Van and then headed into the bathroom. Van turning up unexpectedly was a shock but she had to admit to herself, as she stood under the rapidly warming water, that it was nice to be pursued. She was usually the pursuer. But she had lost the knack after she'd met Sasha. There was no one else she wanted. She knew what Van was offering, and she couldn't deny the attraction, but she wasn't sure she was ready to take that step into intimacy with another woman.

Showered and changed, she found Van sitting on the sofa with Stevie on her lap. They both looked content.

"So, we could go over to the Italian restaurant. They'll be open now and we should be able to get a table at this time."

Van smiled at her and Jamie felt a tingling in her stomach that had nothing to do with being hungry, for food anyway.

"That would be lovely," she said, gently removing Stevie from her lap. He gave her a "you don't really love me" look and padded around in a circle twice before settling down again on the sofa with what sounded like a huff.

Jamie stroked his head and looked at him. "Won't be long, buddy." Stevie accepted this explanation with another heavy sigh and closed his eyes.

The restaurant filled up quickly but they managed to secure a corner table. It was too noisy for much conversation and they made short work of their pasta and salad and two large glasses of red wine, eyeing each other like two cats on heat.

†

Jamie took a roundabout route back from the restaurant to show her the car. Van was suitably impressed. She hadn't owned a car herself since she'd moved into her city apartment. It would have been too expensive to keep and she could get around easily on public transport.

It started to rain before they made it back to the house and they were both soaked by the time they reached the room. Stevie looked at them with disgust and shied away from Jamie's dripping hand when she tried to pet him. He yawned and stretched out to his full length on the sofa.

"I guess that just leaves the bed," Jamie said, laughing. She grabbed Van's hand and led her around the screen.

Van was conscious of her own nipples standing erect but was mesmerised by the sight of Jamie's as she stripped off her shirt. She slowly undid the buttons on her own top without taking her eyes off Jamie as she slipped out of her jeans. They stood facing each other on opposite sides of the mattress like two contestants in a boxing match waiting for the bell. Van felt self conscious in her bra and pants, wishing she had worn something sexier. But she hadn't expected to be removing her clothes in Jamie's presence. And she was stunned by the sight of Jamie's toned body, the small breasts not needing the confines of a bra, muscled shoulders and arms and a six pack that Van could never dream of achieving. This was a scene that had played in Van's mind for several weeks, to see the object of her dreams wearing only a smile and a sexy looking pair of Focx boi shorts.

Jamie walked around the mattress slowly, never taking her eyes off Van. Eyes that seemed to strip her completely. After what seemed like an eternity, Jamie closed the gap between them and reached out to brush a strand of wet hair away from Van's mouth.

"You're so beautiful," Jamie whispered.

Van had never thought of herself as beautiful but to hear the words from the voice that had haunted her dreams and a good number of her waking moments, she believed it.

The first tentative taste of Jamie's lips against hers and she knew that she was lost. She had wanted this from the first time she'd seen this woman. Jamie's strong arms embraced her, pulling her in close so their bodies were touching, skin to skin. Her lips parted to let Jamie's tongue inside, anticipating her desire.

✝

Waking from a deep sleep, Van was dismayed to find the bed empty—apart from the green eyes staring at her from the pillow where Jamie's head had been when she finally drifted off to sleep after the most intense orgasm she'd ever experienced.

"Where's Jamie?" she asked the cat. He blinked and closed his eyes.

Doubts assailed her now, doubts that hadn't been there while Jamie was making love to her. She couldn't complain about Jamie's ardour, she was exceptionally skilled with her hands and tongue. But she had rebutted Van's attempts to reciprocate, not removing her shorts. Butch as she was, Van didn't think she was a classic stone butch. Was this something else she could blame on Sasha? Was that part of Jamie off limits because of her ex's rejection? Another doubt entered her mind. Was Jamie thinking of Sasha when she made love to her, or worse, comparing her to the woman who had dumped her so mercilessly?

Before she could wallow much further into these depressing thoughts she heard footsteps coming quickly up the stairs followed by the door opening and closing

Jamie poked her head around the screen. "You awake?"

Van nodded. Stevie opened his eyes, yawned and stretched.

"Guess he likes you," Jamie moved around the screen and scooped Stevie off the pillow with one easy movement.

She didn't look any less sexy dressed now in jeans and a grey sweatshirt. "You were sound asleep so I've been out for coffee and muffins. Hope that's okay."

Van nodded again. She felt suddenly shy about her nakedness. The night before, in the throes of passion, she hadn't given any thought to the extra pounds she was carrying.

Jamie went into the bathroom, still carrying the cat, and came out with a folded bath towel. She threw it on the bed. "Go on. Have a shower. There's a spare toothbrush in the cabinet. I need to get Stevie's breakfast sorted."

When Van emerged from behind the screen a short while later, fully dressed, hair still damp, Jamie was seated on the sofa, Stevie on her lap, one hand stroking him, the other holding an iPad. Two cardboard coffee cups sat on the crate that served as a table.

Van loved the simple domesticity of the scene. Jamie's look of concentration, the brown eyes scanning whatever was on the screen in front of her—she would have liked to freeze that moment in time.

Sensing her scrutiny, Jamie looked up at her. "Hi. Shower okay? Sorry, I don't have a hair dryer."

"That's all right. As long as you don't mind the shaggy bear look."

Jamie shook her head. "Coffee's still hot. I got yours with milk and one sugar."

Jamie was certainly scoring high on butch points, remembering how she liked her coffee, as well as having a spare, unused toothbrush for her to use. Van walked over to the sofa, unsteady on her feet.

"Chocolate or blueberry? Your choice." Jamie indicated the paper bag on the table.

More points.

"I'll share the blueberry one with you."

Jamie got up and picked up a knife from the bookcase. She pulled off two strips of kitchen roll and brought them over. Splitting the muffin evenly in two, she carefully placed one half on the paper and handed it to Van. Stevie moved up next to her and sniffed at the muffin. It seemed he didn't like blueberry as he jumped off the sofa onto the window ledge.

Van sipped her coffee and found it flavoured perfectly to her taste.

"Sorry, I had to get a move on. The first viewing is at ten on the other side of town. If you don't have any plans for today, would you like to come?"

Looking into Jamie's brown eyes, Van knew she would likely come, again and again. However, she sensed now wasn't the time to make flippant remarks. "Yes, I'd love to."

"Good. It's a nice morning so I was going to walk. After the viewings I thought of taking the car for a spin. There's a great pub over near Haworth where we could have lunch." Jamie's look had intensified. "That's if you want to join me, of course."

After the night they'd shared, Van wondered how she could doubt she would want to spend more time with her. If she ever saw this Sasha woman again, she wouldn't be held responsible for her actions.

"Sounds like a plan."

They finished their coffee and half muffins in companionable silence. Jamie tidied the debris into a black bin liner and placed the spare muffin in her biking backpack.

"I don't think Stevie really would want to eat it, but might as well remove temptation," she said.

Van stood and checked she wasn't wearing any crumbs. "Am I all right like this?" She had dressed for comfort rather than seduction the night before, and had thrown on an old pair of jeans and loose-fitting top in her haste to catch the train.

"We're looking at houses, not going to the Queen's garden party." Jamie moved in close and brushed a few loose strands of hair from her face. "I think you look amazing."

If their kiss could have lasted for eternity, Van was sure she wouldn't have noticed the passing of time. All too soon, Jamie pulled back and gave her a wry smile. "Sorry, but we do have to go now. I would love to spend the rest of the day in bed with you, but if I don't do this today, I'll lose the incentive."

Van followed her down the stairs out onto the street. It was a clear autumn day and when Jamie placed an arm around her shoulders as they walked along, she didn't think she could have felt happier.

Chapter Six

Maddie looked at the girl on the doorstep, hair hanging loose around her shoulders, face puffy from crying. They stared at one another for several minutes. Finally, Maddie took pity on her and stood aside.

"Come in, Annie. It's cold out here."

She preceded her into the living room and sat down in a chair, indicating that Annie should find a seat.

"Dr Hope, I'm really sorry. Can I see Tay? She's not answering her phone."

"Her phone's broken. And she's not really up to seeing anyone at the moment."

More silence as Annie stared at the carpet. Annie, the chubby little girl who had been Tay's playmate since they were four, had turned into quite a beauty, Maddie thought, filling out in all the right places. When her face wasn't blotchy from crying she had clear, rosy skin, the perfect image of an "English rose" with the classic peaches and cream complexion. The doctor was pleased to note she wasn't ruining it with excessive use of cheap cosmetics like a lot of the young girls she saw, some as young as eight.

"What I would like to know, Annie…were you there?" Maddie tried to keep her voice level, very glad that Laurel was out grocery shopping and wouldn't be back for at least an hour. She would have ripped the girl's head off and asked questions later. "Were you with that group of friends who left my daughter puking her guts up in the gutter? Friends who then thought it was funny to take pictures of her, videos even, and leave her there? Friends who then heartlessly walked away laughing? Friends who then texted pictures and posted videos on YouTube? Were you one of those friends, Annie?" She couldn't keep the venom out of her voice every time she used the word "friends."

"No, I wasn't. Honestly, Dr Hope. I wouldn't have left her there."

"She was supposed to be staying over at your house for the night."

"Oh."

"Oh, what? She wasn't staying over at your house?"

"No. I mean she might have meant to come over, but I was out. It was my dad's birthday."

That's easily checked, thought Maddie. Annie's father was one of her patients.

"So, she hadn't arranged to stay the night?"

Annie looked even more miserable, if that was possible, realising no doubt that her answer was getting Taylor into more trouble. She shook her head.

"Is Tay coming back to school?"

"I'm not sure. That's up to her." *And to me,* Maddie added silently.

After some gentle probing Annie confessed that Taylor hadn't arranged to spend the night and was in the habit of asking her friend to cover for her when she was planning to go off with another group.

"Why don't you go with them?"

"It's not my scene."

"What kind of scene is that?"

Annie clammed up. She just shook her head sadly and said they should ask Tay.

Maddie had every intention of doing just that.

The first house they looked at had some nice features, an old stone fireplace in the living room and all the original sash windows. Jamie hadn't said much while they looked around, just nodding politely as the estate agent enthused about its qualities. However, Van didn't need to be a mind reader to know that Jamie wasn't impressed. The house had been on the market for ten months and hadn't been lived in during that time. The owners had moved to France.

When they were walking away, Jamie sighed. "Not quite what I was looking for. It looked better on the website. I don't mind a place that needs a bit of work but that one needed gutting."

"Nice fireplace though."

"Yeah, that was the only redeeming feature."

The second house was more promising. They were shown around by the owner, an elderly man who was moving to be near his daughter's family in Tewkesbury. He'd lived in the house for forty years but it didn't feel the same since his wife died. Although he was sad to leave the place he'd lived in all his life, he was looking forward to spending time with his grandchildren. And Tewkesbury was nice enough, when it wasn't under water. It had suffered badly from the floods the previous year, as part of the town became an island when the River Severn overflowed from the copious amounts of rainfall.

Van discussed the merits of the second house with Jamie on the drive over the moor towards Haworth.

"It will need some work, but mainly just decorating."

"Yes, the wallpaper will definitely have to go." Somehow Van didn't think the large floral prints were Jamie's style.

"It's off the main road and with the woods at the back. I think Stevie will be able to have an outdoor life again. I don't like keeping him cooped up."

Of course, Stevie's comfort was Jamie's primary concern. Van knew that if she wanted a relationship with her it was a matter of "love me, love my cat." Luckily she liked cats and wasn't allergic. And Stevie had accepted her presence, it seemed, without fuss.

"Are you going to make an offer? Mr Corbett seemed keen to move soon."

"I'll talk to the estate agent after lunch. He said he would leave the furnishings, but I don't want to take advantage of the old boy. And I would want to throw it all out anyway. Some of it may well be antique, but not the kind of antiques people pay good money for."

Van had thought the scenery on the drive over was breathtaking, but the sight of the old inn nestled on the roadside, and the welcoming interior with its original old beams and roaring log fire made her feel she'd stepped back in time.

They were shown to a table by the big fireplace. After they'd ordered their drinks and spent a few minutes studying the menu, Jamie leant over and said quietly, "Ivana's a pretty name. Why don't you use it?"

"I don't feel pretty. Just old and frumpy most of the time."

Jamie reached across the table and held her hand. "I wouldn't say that. Old and curvy, maybe," she added, smiling.

"Well, don't you know how to charm a girl? Less of the old, sweet talker."

✝

The drive back took longer as Jamie gave Van the scenic tour through the countryside. She had called the estate agent before they left the Inn's car park. The agent promised to get back to her as soon as possible, but Jamie doubted that would be any time before Monday.

Her phone rang just as they were rounding the last corner down the hill into Hebden Bridge. Jamie had taken the time to set up the Bluetooth when she'd collected the car, so she was able to take the call while driving.

"Hi Maddie."

"Hi, look, sorry to bother you, Jamie. Tay's still not really talked to us but she says she wants to talk to you. We're pretty desperate for some answers. Would you mind coming round?"

"Um. Okay. We're just coming into town."

"Oh, you have someone with you? Sorry. Look, if it's not convenient…"

Jamie could hear the worry in her friend's voice. "No, it's fine. We'll be there in a few minutes."

She ended the call and glanced at Van. "Are you okay with this?"

"Sure. Laurel probably needs some moral support."

Jamie parked behind Maddie's Freelander. She looked over at Van again and reached out to grab one of her hands. "What am I going to say to Taylor? I have no experience with kids."

Van's slate blue eyes had turned a deeper shade of grey. "Don't worry. Sounds like she's the one who'll be doing the talking."

"Why isn't she talking to her parents?"

"Sometimes it's easier to open up to someone not so closely involved."

Jamie held her gaze and moved her other arm to pull herself closer to Van, threading her fingers through her hair. The eyes were drawing her in. "Would you mind if I kissed you?"

"I would mind very much if you didn't."

A few minutes of feasting on those gorgeous lips and tasting Van's sweetness again was all Jamie needed to gather her courage to go and face a traumatised teenager. She pulled back and looked into Van's eyes again. "Will you wait for me?"

"Yes."

Jamie smiled and hopped out quickly, running around the car to open the passenger door.

Van had just managed to unbuckle her seatbelt and looked up at her, surprised. "You don't have to open doors for me."

"I know. But I want to."

They walked up the steps to the front door of the house which opened before they reached it. Maddie welcomed them in.

"She's in the conservatory," she said to Jamie. "Would you like something to drink?"

"Maybe just some water."

"Van?"

"If you've got any juice, that would be great."

"Okay. Laurel's in the living room. I'll bring it through."

Van gave Jamie a quick peck on the cheek. "You'll be fine, sweetheart."

Maddie waited until she'd disappeared into the next room before saying, "Well! You haven't wasted much time."

"Early days." Jamie followed her into the kitchen.

"She's more Laurel's friend than mine, but you could do worse."

"That doesn't sound like much of a recommendation."

Maddie shook her head. "I didn't mean it like that."

Glass of water in hand, Jamie walked into the conservatory and stood in the doorway for a moment. Taylor was sitting on one of the rattan chairs picking at the armrest. Jamie set her glass on the table and pulled up another chair to face the girl. Her hair was hanging limply around her face. It didn't look like it had been washed in days. This was a different person to the confident youngster who had flirted with her so outrageously only a few weeks before.

"So, what's up?" she asked, when it didn't look like Tay was going to speak first.

"Everyone hates me."

"That's not true. Your parents love you."

"No they don't. Not like Leo. He's never done anything wrong. And then he goes and dobs me in."

"Well, I think he loves you too. He doesn't want to see you hurt. That's why he alerted them. What if I hadn't found you? Who would have stopped to help you? Your parents would have been frantic, searching the streets. He was looking out for you. It was the best he could do, being so far away."

"Do you have a brother?"

Jamie looked out into the garden. "Yes. But he was younger than me."

"Did you get on?"

"When he was little it was okay. But I wasn't happy with him trailing around after me when I was older."

"Are you close now?"

"I wish."

"What happened?"

"He's dead. Died in Afghanistan. A bomb. There wasn't enough of him left to bring home."

Taylor looked at her for the first time, tears showing on her cheeks. "Oh, wow. That's awful."

Jamie looked away again, close to tears herself. This time of year leading up to Remembrance Day was hard, when people started wearing poppies. Not that she or her parents ever forgot about Josh.

She looked back at the girl. "So, you never know what's going to happen. Treasure what you've got."

They sat in silence for a few more minutes. Jamie sipped her water and waited.

"I can't go back to school," Taylor stated eventually.

"Well, it didn't seem like you wanted to be there anyway. What do you want to do?"

131

"I don't know. I'm useless."

"I doubt that's true. There must be something you like doing. Or something you've always wanted to do. You've got your whole life ahead of you, and believe me, Tay, you only get one shot at it. So make the most of it."

"Mum says you've had a hard time getting over your breakup, you know…"

"Well, that's the whole point. I am getting over it. Sometimes it takes more time than you would like. But you get there in the end, if you stick at it."

They both stared at the table for a few minutes.

"Why did you want to talk to me, and not your parents?"

"It's just…I can't…"

"Have you told them about your feelings for your friend, Shaz, wasn't it?"

"No."

"You've been brought up by two lesbians. What could be hard about talking to them?"

"That's just it. Do you know how much shit I've had to put up with at school? People asking me who my dad is? Jokes about sperm banks and turkey basters. I just wanted to fit in."

"So is that what all the stuff was with the make-up and the girly outfits."

"Yeah. But I could never seem to get it right. I mean, I just wanted to be normal."

"What's normal? It's much better to just be yourself and not try to fit into what you think other people expect. You're so lucky. A lot of the kids at school will have horrible home lives. Like I said before, you have two very loving parents. They will support you, whatever you do. And right now they're hurting because you won't confide in them. How do you think they feel, knowing you would rather talk to someone who's a virtual stranger, rather than them? Give them a chance, Tay."

The girl nodded.

"All this crap…the drinking, smoking, whatever…it's not important. Your happiness is what matters to them."

They sat in silence for a bit longer, each immersed in their thoughts. Jamie didn't know if her words helped Tay at all. Talking about Josh brought up more memories than she wanted to deal with right then.

✝

Van sat down next to Laurel and took her hands. Her eyes, normally clear blue, were bloodshot with bags weighing heavily under them. Van had never seen Laurel look anything but stunningly beautiful. She'd often joked about the painting she must have hidden in the attic. But now she couldn't think of anything to say that would comfort her friend.

Maddie came in and set a glass of juice on the table in front of her. Taking the chair opposite she said, "So, you and Jamie…"

"Yes, I stayed the night with her if that's what you want to know."

"Great. I guess Sasha's finally consigned to history."

"I hope so." Van let go of Laurel's hands and sat back. The early morning doubts returned. But she shook her head, remembering the fervour of Jamie's kiss in the car and the way her serious brown eyes caressed her when she said "will you wait for me?"

133

A mobile phone buzzed. Maddie reached over and picked it up.

"It's Leo, love," she said, addressing Laurel. She looked down at the message. "The train's just left Tod, so he'll be here soon."

Laurel looked up. "Oh. I better go and freshen up." She stood quickly and left the room.

Maddie sighed. "Always Leo. No wonder Tay thinks she hates her."

Van stood as well. "I'll go and wait in the car. This is obviously family business."

"No, stay. I don't know how long they'll be. Although Jamie's definitely succeeding where we've failed." She looked at her watch. "We haven't been able to get more than a few words out of her since that evening."

"How's Leo doing with his course?" Van sat down again and took a sip of her juice.

"From what I gather, not much has started yet. He's still finding his way around the campus. But he seems to be settling in okay. He wasn't due to come home this weekend but he's worried about his sister."

"I thought they didn't get on."

"She probably doesn't realise it, but he's always been very protective of her."

✝

Jamie stood and held out her hand. "Come on, kiddo. Time to face the music."

The girl gave her a small smile and took her hand. She seemed unsteady on her feet.

134

"You need some exercise. Too much lying around feeling sorry for yourself."

"I'm okay."

"Sure you are. Ready now?"

Tay nodded and followed her through the kitchen and down the hall to the living room. The voices in the room stopped when they entered and three faces looked up at them.

Jamie didn't know who was more surprised when Leo jumped to his feet and rushed over to engulf his sister in a hug. And the look on Laurel's face as she entered the room was priceless.

Catching Van's eyes, Jamie motioned with her head and walked out.

Closing the front door behind them, Van let out a big sigh.

"She'll be okay, won't she?"

"Yes. She just needs to know how lucky she is, and it looks like that might be making an impression now."

"So, you didn't have any trouble talking to her."

"I was a teenager once. I wouldn't want to go through that again for anything."

"Too right."

Jamie opened the passenger door of the car for Van and waited until she'd seated herself before closing it. She sat behind the wheel for a few minutes. Talking to Taylor had brought up some emotions she didn't want to deal with right now. Memories of Josh were never far from her mind, even after eight years.

"Are you okay?"

Rubbing her hands over her face, Jamie let out a deep breath. She started the car. "Yeah." There was only one place to go now that would help to dispel her gloomy thoughts. But she wanted to be on her own.

†

Sitting back in her seat, Van wasn't sure what had just happened. One minute she thought she was going back to Jamie's place for more hot sex, the next she was being dropped off at the train station.

Well, she did need a change of clothes after the night and day she'd just had, but she would have liked to know what was going on. Jamie had just said she needed some time on her own. She said she would call.

†

The walk by the river helped, and finding her quiet spot to sit listening to the water rushing past, and watching a heron sitting as still as herself on the opposite bank, had calmed her thoughts.

When Leo had embraced his sister so warmly, she had been assaulted by the image of her last sight of Josh. He had spent a few days with their parents and stopped by to see her on his way back to rejoin his unit. They were flying out to Afghanistan the next day. He hadn't wanted to go. Having spent some time in Iraq, he wasn't keen on another desert posting and joining a fight they weren't likely to win.

She had just started seeing Sasha and was full of the excitement of a new relationship, giving Josh more information than he needed about the wonderful woman she'd met. But he had listened and hugged her, saying he was pleased for her. Their five-year age difference, which had seemed huge when they were children, had melted away to nothing, and as adults they discovered a deepening friendship. Josh's decision to join the army surprised and dismayed their parents, but he knew early on that he wasn't cut out for an academic career. His hyperactivity at school had seen him labelled as ADHD from his second year in primary school. She remembered how upset he'd been to find out on his first day at high school that he was on the special needs register. Jamie had done her best to reassure him that it was just the school's way of getting extra funding and he wasn't alone. It didn't mean he was any thicker than anyone else. She'd told him to do as many sports as he could and not to worry about any of the other shit.

When he told her he was joining up she had been proud of him. And he'd done well. Although he was nervous about going into a war zone again, he was excited at the same time. He had just been told he would be trained to fly helicopters. It was a boyhood dream come true.

Jamie sighed. The rushing water didn't hold any answers and the heron had flown off. In a way, Josh had achieved his dream and she was wallowing around in a dead-end job because of a failed love life. Her brother wouldn't have wanted to see her like this. He would have "kicked her ass" as he'd learned to say when dealing with new squaddies. She needed to buck up her thinking and quick. Buying the car and looking at houses was a start. She stood up. Since she was walking back into town, she would stop at the estate agents and make an offer on Mr Corbett's house.

Back at home, with Stevie in her arms and the cat sensing she needed his affection, she realised she should phone Van. That is, if the poor woman wanted to speak to her. What was she thinking, practically shoving her onto the train?

She stared at her phone as if it could tell her what to do. After a few more minutes of indecision she told it to phone Van and picked it up when it started ringing. It went on to voicemail.

"Hi. Look, I'm sorry. I…" Jamie floundered over the words to say for the recording. Van's voice broke in before she could think of anything else.

"Jamie! Are you okay?"

"Better now."

"What happened?"

To Jamie's relief Van didn't sound angry, just concerned.

"Talking to Taylor brought up some memories from the past. I just needed some time to deal with them."

"Do you want to talk about it?"

"No. Yeah, I don't know." Jamie would have liked to sound more mature but realised she was giving a good impression of a ten-year-old.

"I've just got in, but I could come back this evening, if you want me to."

"I'd like that but surely you don't want to trek out here again."

"Well, my plans for this evening consisted of washing my hair and beating some kid from China on *FIFA 15* to the top spot."

Jamie laughed. "Okay. But if you don't mind staying in, I'll get a takeaway."

"Sure, that works for me."

"Indian, Thai or Pizza?

"Let's go Thai."

"Um, tomorrow though, I've got a hill assessment with the Search and Rescue team so I'll be out most of the day."

"That's okay. The town looks to have lots of interesting little shops and cafés. I'm sure I can amuse myself for a few hours."

Van checked the train timetable and said she could be there about half past eight. That gave her time to do a few things at home before setting off again.

Jamie sank back into the sofa and closed her eyes. It had been quite a day and it wasn't over yet.

✝

The dream sequences wouldn't leave her alone. There was a power there, drawing her in. Phoebe didn't understand how Sasha couldn't share this with her. Philip Pearlman, though, he understood. She could see the passion in his eyes when he talked her through the changes he thought she should make.

She contemplated the page in front of her; Philip told her this passage had power.

When the Merlin first gave her the harp and told her to play, she said she didn't know how. The Merlin said she would know. The knowledge was in her blood.

As she played, in her mind's eye she could see the circle of stones moving, clumsily at first, then more gracefully as if following the steps in a dance. Gradually, as the music filled her being, the walls of the cave fell away and she was aware of playing in a vast space above the shadowy green and blue centre of the planet's surface. And with her came the stones, the circle still intact, and as she watched they became dancing figures reaching out to one another, weaving in and out as a chain in an endless spiralling motion. The rhythm changed and as they came closer with their swirling movements, she could see faces—bright, laughing faces. Moments, or hours, later the spell was broken with the return of the Merlin—and the confines of the cave walls reasserted themselves.

"Very fine, Alethea," the Merlin said in a calm, measured tone. "Your playing has improved."

†

"Bring it to life for me, Phoebe," he had urged. "Make the stones talk. The music of the spheres, the magic of the stars, it's all there. I know you can do this."

And she believed she could. But she needed to feel the energy, breathe in the air, hear the music rippling through the breeze. A trip to Stonehenge was out of the question and too touristy now, but there were other henges. Britain was littered with stone circles. What was the closest moorland? A quick Google search and she found her location. A short train journey away, she could book into a local B&B for a few nights.

The whole area was alive with wonderfully evocative names—Crimsworth Dean, Pecket Well, Robin Hood's Penny Stone, and tellingly, Han Royd Earth Circle—a landscape with many stories to tell.

There was no point letting Sasha know what she was doing, she would only come up with reasons why she shouldn't do it. And she couldn't expect her to understand really. She'd spent months agonising over the words of this story, a story she wanted to tell. She was bored with her life of crime. It was fantasy all the way now. And she was going to make it work.

The romance of the adventure took over and she started to plan.

Chapter Seven

Van arrived at her desk out of breath. Leaving Jamie's bed at 6:30, she thought there was plenty of time to get back to her flat, shower, and change. But, of course, one train had been cancelled and the one she was on was crammed full with other desperate commuters. A quick strip wash was all she had time for at home. As she stood in front of the bathroom mirror frantically combing through the tangles in her hair all she could smell was the overpowering evidence of another night spent with a very active lover.

If she'd been thinking straight at all when Jamie called her back on Saturday, she would have planned it properly, and packed more than one change of underwear as well as the security pass she needed to get into the building for work.

Computer on, she took a deep breath and hoped she could persuade Connor to get her a cup of coffee. The stuff from the machine was vile but it would have to do until her lunch break.

Her thoughts were still overwhelmed with the events of the last few days—and nights. How could she forget the nights? Just the memory of Jamie's hands on her breasts with the quirky smile that meant she was thinking of licking her nipples and moving her hands further down—Van thought she was going to melt into her chair.

"Hey, Earth to Van!"

She looked up to see the boy's smiling face hanging over the screen, his ears pink from the cold outside.

"Must have been good." He gave her a suggestive leer.

"It was. And if you want any details, you'll have to be nice to an old lady and bring her a cup of coffee. No, make it two."

"Ooh. Wow. Awesome. Don't go away." He scampered off.

The energy of youth. Mind you, Jamie had more than enough energy. She'd been getting ready to cycle to work. Van asked why she didn't take the new car and Jamie said it was only for bad weather days, a bit of rain didn't count.

As she typed out routine answers to the questions customers constantly asked, her mind wandered. After their first lovemaking session on Saturday evening, Van had asked if Jamie was having her period.

She had looked at her blankly. "I haven't had a period in over a year."

"Oh. Well, I just wondered. I really want to touch you, to taste you."

Jamie was still wearing her briefs. She had fallen back onto her pillow and sighed deeply.

"I'm sorry. I just, well you make me feel so good. I want to return the favour."

143

After a few more sighs, Jamie propped herself up on her elbow and looked at her. She licked her lips and Van felt her clit pulsing. Just the thought of Jamie's tongue on her and she was getting wet again. For another long moment she didn't think Jamie was going to say anything. And when she did, it wasn't what she expected.

"I had an abnormal result on my last smear test. I'm waiting now for the results of the hospital tests I had done a few weeks ago. Until I know if I'm clear, I'd rather not, you know…"

"Oh, okay." Van had looked into the anxious brown eyes. "But, if there was anything seriously wrong, I'm sure they would have let you know by now. Can't Maddie find out for you?"

"She said she'd look into it."

Van placed a hand on Jamie's flat stomach. She could feel the tension there. Her fingers travelled onto the briefs. "How about if I promise to only look. It would be so good to feel your skin against mine."

She was just getting to the part where Jamie had removed the offending item and let her put her hand on the soft mound with its tantalising bush of curly hair, when Connor returned and put the two cups of coffee on her desk.

"Break time. All the details." He disappeared behind the screen.

Van sighed. The moment was gone. She had a feeling the day was going to seem longer than usual.

†

It was a relief to sit in her office waiting for the first patient of the day. The weekend had been an emotional time for all of them. Leo's arrival and overt show of affection for his sister had opened the floodgates.

Taylor told them how she felt about the girl in her class, and had since the first time she'd seen her. And how her decision to finally let her know by kissing her in public had led to the unfortunate chain of events that resulted in Tay ending up face down in a gutter Wednesday evening. She figured all her friends hated her now. Maddie told her about Annie's visit and that she was seeing the head teacher at the school Monday morning. She reassured her daughter that they weren't going to force her to go back until she felt ready.

It had taken all three of them to convince Taylor that all she needed to do was be herself. She had been trying too long to be someone else. And if she felt the urge to kiss someone, maybe it would be a good idea to do it privately and with that person's consent.

Tay had rallied at that point, saying to Leo, "What do you know about it, dork? You've never had a girlfriend."

In Maddie's early morning meeting with the head teacher, he had assured her that any bullying would be dealt with appropriately. He understood if Taylor felt she needed to take more time off school. Her teachers could send work home. He would let the head of the sixth form know.

It was hard for Maddie to feel any rapport with the man. He didn't live locally and his expectations for the students didn't fit with the culture of the valley. She didn't feel she could tell him that his anti-bullying policy sucked. And that maybe they should be having assemblies on tackling homophobia rather than what Taylor had described as mind-numbingly boring motivational speeches by successful ex-pupils. Laurel wouldn't have held back from speaking her mind if she'd come with her. But her wife had stayed at home, having breakfast with Leo before he set off to catch the mid-morning train.

Maddie smiled, remembering the night before. For the first time in what seemed like months, Laurel had initiated intimate contact. She had snuggled up to her and playfully tweaked one of her breasts before whispering in her ear, "I'm going to ravish you, quietly." Not that either of the kids, plugged into their devices, would have heard them.

†

Jamie enjoyed the ride to work and the time it gave her to think about the weekend. When she'd started cycling shortly after moving to Hebden Bridge, Maddie had told her she was nuts. She could have rented somewhere nearer to the university. It was over an hour's ride each way and the traffic on the busy roads was downright dangerous at times. The first few weeks had been hard but she'd stuck at it even though she initially arrived at each destination with legs trembling and bottom aching. The padded shorts she'd invested in after the first week had felt odd initially, but were certainly a butt-saver.

A punishing ride, Maddie had called it. What was she punishing herself for—being a lousy girlfriend, getting dumped for a younger model, not fighting back, losing Stevie?

Well she was in better shape now than she'd ever been. She had Stevie back and she had a girlfriend. Being with Van was fun. She enjoyed her natural warmth and humour. And she was incredibly sexy in bed.

The hill assessment with the Search and Rescue people had gone well. They thought she would make a great addition to the team. Van had been happy when they met up later, having enjoyed the busy Sunday in the small town with its village community-like atmosphere, the square filling up with cyclists and ramblers and street artists. Van had visited the craft fair and walked along by the canal. It was like being on holiday in a foreign country she'd told Jamie, a mere twenty-five miles from Manchester.

And, to top it all, sometime today she would hear whether or not her offer on the house had been accepted. Jamie was paying cash, so with no chain involved, as long as the survey didn't show up any major problems, there was a good chance she could be moving soon.

There was no sign of Mike or Jonathan in the office when she arrived. Jamie started the coffee maker going and went down the hall to change out of her lycra. When she got back, the coffee was ready but still no sign of the guys. While she waited for her computer to boot up, she checked the whiteboard for any clues. Nothing new. Just the reminder for the staff meeting from two months ago and a big circle around "Check library monitors," a task she and Mike had completed during the summer break.

She poured herself a mug of coffee and sat down to read her emails. There was only one from Friday, sent after she'd left for the day. It was from the head of HR's secretary asking her to attend a meeting. She stared at it. The meeting was for 9:30 today. It was now 9:15. Damn. The only time she'd visited the Human Resources department was on her induction, eight months earlier. She looked at the campus plan taped to the wall behind her screen. Not too far away.

She should be able to make it there in time without breaking into a sweat.

Walking quickly down the corridor, she wondered what it was about. As far as she knew, HR wouldn't be involved in her request for a parking permit. That was between Admin and Security. She didn't think she'd committed any misdemeanours unless someone objected to her changing her clothes in the toilet. She hadn't left any smelly socks or other pungent cycling garments on the radiator.

A young man with a straggly beard met her at the door when she appeared.

"Jamie Steele?"

"Yes."

"Good. This way, please."

Jamie followed him through the maze of desks in the open-plan office space. Well-trained staff. They all had their heads down, looking busy, even if they weren't. At least two of them were texting under their desks. At least, that's what she hoped they were doing.

The woman seated behind the executive-sized desk in the only enclosed office didn't look up when she was shown in. Her computer screen showed a picture of a younger woman and baby. Daughter and grandchild, Jamie guessed. The desk itself was clear of clutter, just the open file the woman was studying. Jamie sat down in the one chair facing the desk.

When the woman did look up, her clear blue eyes seemed to bore into Jamie. She didn't bother with introductions, probably assuming Jamie knew who she was. A sudden smile appeared and her face was transformed from steely executive mode to caring employer.

"Jamie, glad you could make it at such short notice. Would you like a coffee?"

"No thanks. I've just had some."

"You're probably wondering what this is about so I'll come straight to the point." Her face looked grim again as the smile disappeared. "Jonathan Fremantle has left us in a bit of mess. He resigned on Friday."

"Really?" No wonder he'd been happy to let her go off early.

"Yes. We knew he was having some difficulties at home and had given him extra leave days to try and sort things out. Anyway, he's gone."

"Doesn't he have to work out his notice?"

"That would have been the usual procedure. But in this case, he wanted to leave with immediate effect, and as he's been absent so much lately, it seemed like the best option for both parties." She paused, looking down at the papers in front of her again. "That leaves us with his position to fill. I've been reviewing your application. You seem rather over-qualified for the job you're currently doing."

"I like it." Jamie didn't think she needed to give her reasons for taking the job.

"That's good. We would like to offer you the position as head of IT Services."

Jamie looked down at the floor.

"It's quite a jump in salary scale, more in line with what you would have been used to, I think."

"Don't you have to advertise the job, at least internally?"

"In this case there isn't anyone on staff remotely qualified. There are some big projects coming up which will need someone with your expertise."

Jamie knew she was referring to the upgrade of the online learning system, something Jonathan had been putting off since before she'd arrived on the scene.

"We will, of course, be advertising for another technician so you won't be short-staffed."

"If I agree to take this job, the first thing I would ask for is an additional technician. We're short-staffed as it is. And the office space really isn't adequate."

The woman smiled. "I think that can be arranged. Can I take that as a 'yes'?"

Jamie sighed. She knew it was the right thing to do. She'd been drifting along and now things were coming together in ways she hadn't foreseen even a few weeks ago.

"Does Mike know you're offering this to me? I haven't been here very long. He should be the next in line."

"We've talked to him. He's perfectly happy for you to take over the reins. He knows he doesn't have the right experience yet."

"Well, I think he should be given a raise. With two new assistants, he'll need to train them. He's ready for more responsibility."

"You drive a hard bargain, Miss Steele, but I think we can accommodate your demands."

Jamie stood. "Those are just the start. I expect you'll be sending me the outcome of this discussion in writing."

The smile on the other woman's face widened. She got to her feet as well and reached her hand across the desk. Jamie shook it.

"Count on it. I'll have the revised contracts sent over to your office today. A pleasure doing business with you."

The walk back to the IT Services office didn't seem as long as it had half an hour earlier. Her mind was whirling through all the things that needed to be done. Things that Jonathan had let slide. She'd taken the technician's job to get herself through her own problems, fighting the despair that Sasha's betrayal had left. She hadn't cared enough to find out why Jonathan wasn't doing his job properly. It had just been a matter of getting through each day without breaking down during the first few months.

She was still in a daze when she walked through the door and was startled by Mike's greeting, "Hey, boss! Way to go."

He was grinning at her and pointing to a box on her desk. "I know you don't normally indulge, but I got these to celebrate your promotion."

Jamie looked in the box. Two pastries, one apple strudel, one walnut Danish. "How did you know I would take it? I might have said no."

"Well, if you hadn't, we could have celebrated our ex-leader's departure."

"It was very sudden. He didn't say anything to you, did he?"

"No. But who cares. The king is dead, long live the queen."

Jamie smiled at him. His enthusiasm was catching. "I'm not sure I want to be a queen. Anyway, we have two promotions to celebrate. You're my new deputy and you will shortly have two techies to train."

"Awesome. Oh wow! If I'd known, I would have got a cake."

†

Sasha tripped over the suitcase in the hallway and swore. She switched on the light and was surprised to see the clutter surrounding the case. Walking boots, anorak, backpack, Ordnance Survey map in a waterproof cover. WTF? Clearance sale at the camping shop, or what? Her lover never walked anywhere unless it involved a trip to Harvey Nicks when she would happily traverse each floor looking for a bargain.

It didn't look like Phoebe was leaving her. More than one suitcase would have been needed to empty her portion of the wardrobe.

She called out, "Feebs?"

"In the kitchen."

Sasha walked down the hallway and was greeted with the sight of Phoebe's black lace panties barely covering her behind as she bent over scrabbling through a cupboard. Tamping down the surge of desire, Sasha asked, "What are you looking for?"

Phoebe stood up, her hair in disarray, flushed, with sweat beads forming on her face. "I thought we had a thermos."

"We had to throw it out. The bottom had rusted away."

"Oh, right. Well, I guess I can buy one when I get there."

"Get where? I didn't know you were going anywhere." Sasha had postponed an author meeting to be home early in the hopes of initiating another romantic evening. And seeing her lover wearing nothing more than skimpy black underwear, she thought perhaps that's what Phoebe had planned as well.

Phoebe leant back against the counter and Sasha swallowed at the sight of her erect nipples poking through the black lace. "Well, Philip suggested I need more authentic sounding detail about the stone circle in the book."

Sasha closed her eyes. Why couldn't the creep just have told her the book was shit and leave it alone? This was taking competition to a whole new level. She opened her eyes and made herself focus on Phoebe's face. "You can surely get what you need online. You don't go out and kill someone when you write a murder mystery."

"Sarcasm doesn't suit you. Of course, I can get a basic description and look at photos online. But I want to feel the atmosphere, hear the wind howling around…"

"I hope you weren't planning to go dressed like that. The wind will be howling up your crotch."

"No need to be vulgar. This is important to me, Sash, but I can't expect you to care, can I? You're still mooning over what's-her-name."

"I'm not mooning." Sasha took the few steps that brought her close to Phoebe. She placed her hands around her waist. "You're more than enough woman for me."

"I wish I could believe that."

"How about I show you?" Sasha pulled her close and kissed her firmly.

†

Laurel looked around the table, satisfied. Taylor was joining them for the evening meal having just said goodbye to Annie. The girls had spent the afternoon together in Tay's room. When Maddie went to check on them before dinner, they were sitting cross-legged on the bed facing each other, playing a card game.

"How did the meeting with the head go?" Laurel asked, passing the salad bowl to Maddie.

"Oh, he made all the right noises. Says he's fine with Tay taking more time off school. Her teachers will send work home and he'll let the head of sixth form know."

"That twat."

"Hey, language, sweetheart."

"Well, he is a…"

"All right, enough. I don't know him but I'm sure he does his best."

"Yeah, right." Taylor poked a tomato out of the way.

"Well, as we said yesterday, you do have other options. You don't have to go back at all. There are sixth form colleges. Depending on what courses you want to take, there may still be places available."

"Or I could join the army. Annie says Callum Bates did and he's loving it."

"You're not Callum Bates." Laurel couldn't keep the tone of disapproval out of her voice. Callum was well known as having a track record of being excluded from school for long periods of time. The army was the best place for him in her opinion.

"Okay. The navy, then."

"Tay, be serious. You don't even know how to swim."

"I can learn."

"The law says you have to stay in some form of education until you're eighteen."

"How about the police?"

This discussion wasn't going as planned but at least Tay was looking better and sounding more like her usual self. Laurel wouldn't have thought she would welcome the return of Tay's bolshie teenage attitude, however she was glad to see it reasserting itself now.

†

Connor wasn't happy at being fobbed off with a general outline of the weekend's activities. He wasn't interested in detailed descriptions of the delights of the country inn where they'd had lunch, or the little shops she'd wandered in and out of on Sunday while Jamie was out. He picked up on the one thing he thought was significant.

"You went house-hunting with her! Wow! That's quick work. I've heard about lesbians moving in together after the first date, but buying a house together, that's well wicked."

"We're not buying a house together. She's buying a house."

"And you're going to move in with her."

"No. We're just dating."

"Is that what you call it? Three nights of hot sex isn't 'just dating'."

"Who said anything about hot sex."

"You don't have to, you. You're glowing so brightly we should plug you into the national grid."

"Oh, shut up. What do you know about it?" She checked her watch. "We need to get back before the boss sends out a search party."

Back at their respective desks, Van made an effort to look like she was concentrating on her work. When their lunch break came around, she quickly scuttled off to the Ladies and sat in a cubicle to check her phone. It had vibrated several times but she hadn't been able to look at it with their supervisor making his rounds at regular intervals during the morning.

Three texts from Jamie. All good news. She'd got a promotion at work and her offer on the house had been accepted. But the most newsworthy from Van's point of view, Maddie had rung to say she'd tracked down her test results. All clear and the letter was on its way to her.

She decided to risk phoning her. Jamie picked up on the second ring.

"Congratulations. Brilliant news all round."

"Yeah. Almost as good as winning the lottery. Look, I know we agreed to meet up Wednesday, but I'm going to be busy with this new job. I think it would be better if we left it until Friday. Sorry."

Not as sorry as I am, thought Van. *A whole fucking week, without fucking.* And now she knew the coast was clear, so to speak, she was looking forward to giving Jamie a great deal of pleasure in that area.

"Okay."

"I know. I am sorry. But we have been left with a bit of a mess here by my predecessor. Anyway, I'll call you this evening. Bye."

That was it. Well she needed to sort a few things out at home herself. Her flat was a mess with a good week's worth of neglect. Laundry to do. Grocery shopping. Back to reality. But she could hold on to the fact that Jamie wanted to see her Friday and maybe they could indulge in some phone sex this evening. Connor was right. This wasn't "just dating." For her, anyway, this was the start of something more.

†

Sasha was still asleep when Phoebe left the house on Tuesday morning. It was dark outside. The note she'd left on the kitchen table gave Sasha details of where she was staying; it wasn't like she was running away. It was only a few days of exploration, and she would be back.

It took several trips to pack her gear into the car. Suitcase, backpack, boots, outdoor clothing, Kendal mint cakes, and bottles of energy drinks. She ticked the items off her list. This hiking business was exhausting and she hadn't even trekked anywhere yet. Satisfied nothing had been left behind, she backed the car slowly out of the driveway and headed off down the street. A sense of release came over her as the iPod picked up in the middle of the last track she'd played—Amy McDonald singing "Life in a Beautiful Light" with feeling. It matched her mood as she swung the car out onto the main road and headed for the hills.

The night before had brought back memories of their first lust-filled times together. She loved it when Sasha took charge and made love to her with such intensity. That passion had been lacking before, so maybe she was winning. Not that she gave a shit what Sasha's mates thought of her, but she knew they all agreed she was a much better match for their friend than that boring geek, Jamie.

A few days away and Sasha would be begging for it once more. She could feel her lover's fingers inside her and her clit throbbed with the memory of their recent lovemaking. "Give it a rest," she told herself, sternly. If her thoughts carried on like this she'd be stopping by the side of the road to satisfy herself with the gear stick.

†

With a few minutes of peace before the next patient, Maddie chewed on the remnants of her tuna sandwich and scrolled through the news items on the BBC website. Gloom and doom everywhere. The sports section wasn't much better. If Manchester United didn't improve their back line soon they would be lucky to stay out of the relegation zone.

The door opened and she didn't turn around, expecting it to be Janet bringing in the supply of sterile pads she'd asked for.

"Mads?"

She looked up from the screen, startled. "Tay? What are you…?"

"Janet said it was okay to come through. Your next patient cancelled."

"Oh, right." Maddie swivelled her chair round to face her daughter. "Have a seat, sweetie. Is this a medical consultation?"

"No." Taylor looked down at her feet.

Maddie waited. Unlike Laurel, she knew that silence on her part was a good way to get Tay to speak.

"I don't want to go back to school."

"Okay."

"I was sort of serious last night. I know I'm not cut out for university. I'm not like Leo."

"No one expects you to be like Leo."

"I do want to join the army. I looked it up. I'm fit enough. My GCSE grades are good enough. For the first part

158

of the training, I would be based at Harrogate. That's not so far, is it?"

Maddie looked back at her screen. This was going to be difficult to sell to Laurel. Although the British Army was now withdrawn from Afghanistan, there was talk of them going back. And there were plenty of other trouble spots in the world where troops could be deployed. She looked back at Taylor. The girl had a determined look on her face that she hadn't seen for some time.

"Will you talk to Mum for me?"

'I don't like the idea any more than she will, but if it's what you really want to do, we won't stand in your way."

"Okay. Great." The girl gave her a brief smile and looked down at her feet again.

"Is there something else?"

"Um, yeah."

Another long pause. Maddie waited. She didn't know what she was going to say if Tay told her she was pregnant. It would be disappointing, to say the least, after all the talks they'd had on the subject. Much to Laurel's chagrin, Maddie hadn't shied away from giving both their children all the information she thought they could handle from an early age. But, of course, they would support her if she wanted to have the baby. With these thoughts going through her mind, Maddie was totally unprepared for her daughter's next words.

Tay looked up at her, eyes filled with tears. "I want to know who my father is."

†

The day had been long and there were times when she wondered why she'd agreed to take on the job, but by six o'clock she felt like she had a better grip on what needed to be done. Prioritising their workload, she delegated writing the job description for the new techs to Mike. After all, it was his job. As she'd suspected he would, he sucked up the responsibility without any fuss.

Towards the end of the afternoon, she realised Jonathan hadn't done anything about her parking permit request. She had talked to both Admin and Security and was told it would be ready for her the next day. Checking the weather, she thought she'd probably cycle in, but it would be good to have the option of bringing the car.

She hadn't had time to mull over her phone call with Van until she was cycling home. She knew that Van was disappointed at having to wait longer before their next meeting. She was going to need to get a decent night's sleep for a few nights and Van was a serious distraction in bed.

Stevie greeted her with his usual affectionate meow, winding himself through her legs, angling for a cuddle. She picked him up and gazed into his green eyes. "Things are looking up, Stevie boy. But I think we'll celebrate with a quiet night in. Hope you haven't finished off the wine."

He purred softly. She took that as a "no," and placed him carefully on the bed before heading into the bathroom for a shower.

The phone rang while she was towelling off. She picked it up from the top of the bookcase. Maddie.

"Hi."

"Hi. Are you at home?"

"Yeah, just got back."

"Look, I know this is a bit of an imposition, but do you think you could come round?"

"Um, like now?"

"Yes. I wouldn't ask if it wasn't important."

"Has something happened to Taylor?"

"It concerns her, but no. Nothing physical anyway."

Jamie put the phone down after agreeing to be there shortly. She looked at Stevie. He'd moved to his favourite spot on the sofa. "So much for our quiet night in."

†

Maddie put the phone down. "She's coming over."

Laurel put her head in her hands. "Why now? Why does Taylor want to know now?"

"It was likely to happen sometime."

"Leo's never shown any interest."

"He might when he finds out Taylor knows who her father is."

Laurel put some cheese and crackers on a plate. "Will this do?"

"She's just got in from work, so I guess it will be okay. Have we got some red wine?"

"Yes, I've put it out."

They went through to the living room. Taylor was checking out the apps on her new phone. She looked up. "I'm full."

"This isn't for you. Jamie's coming round."

"Oh. Why?"

Maddie sat down next to her. "Because…well, you'll find out when she gets here."

The discussion earlier about Taylor's career choice had been tense. Laurel, as Maddie predicted, wasn't happy with the idea. But as it was the first time Tay had shown any interest in planning for her future, she'd finally agreed to let her at least give it a try.

The doorbell rang and Maddie went to let Jamie in.

"Would you like some wine?" she asked leading the way into the room.

Jamie nodded.

"The cheese and biscuits are for you. We've already eaten, but we thought you might want something."

"Thanks." Jamie sat down in one of the easy chairs. Laurel placed a glass of wine on the table next to the chair along with the plate.

When she'd sat back down, Maddie said, "Taylor wants to know who her father is. And I have to say that until today we didn't know the name of the donor." She held up a brown envelope. "Until this evening, this envelope has stayed sealed in my filing cabinet, for the time when Tay might want to meet her father. When we applied for a donor, we only asked to see a photograph of the man and were given details on his health, blood type, that kind of thing. He fitted all our criteria. And it helped that he was blond and blue-eyed. We thought he looked a lot like Laurel, and although I'm Taylor's birth mother, that's how she's turned out." Holding up a second envelope, she said, "This is the photograph we have." She handed the envelope to Jamie.

Taylor was on the edge of her seat now.

Jamie took the envelope and pulled out the photo. It was a small print, four by three. She swallowed. "Josh."

Tay grabbed the photo out of her hand.

"We honestly didn't know, Jamie." Maddie looked down at the other envelope in her hands. "This gives his name. I remember you saying you have a younger brother. We weren't sure about contacting him or if he would even want to know he has a daughter. We thought, well, we wanted to ask if you would talk to him first, sound him out."

"It would be difficult." Jamie took a gulp of her wine. "He died eight years ago."

Taylor looked up from staring at the image in front of her. "This is the brother you told me about."

"Yes."

"He doesn't look anything like you."

"I know. We used to joke about Mum having slept with the milkman or that the babies were switched at the hospital."

"Have you got other photos of him?"

"Sure." She pulled her phone out of her pocket.

Maddie held onto Laurel's hand as they watched their daughter intently studying the photos Jamie was showing her on the small screen.

"That was taken just before he left for Afghanistan. His promotion to Captain had come through. And that's the last one he sent us, standing next to the helicopter he was learning to fly."

"Wow. That's awesome." Taylor looked up at Jamie. "This means you're my aunt, doesn't it?"

"Yeah, I guess it does."

Tay smiled and looked back at the picture on the phone, Josh's smile for the camera mirroring her own.

†

It was after eleven when Jamie got back to her room. Stevie woke up briefly to acknowledge her entrance, then settled down again.

The evening had brought back so many memories, some almost too painful to share. But Taylor was keen to know everything about her newly discovered father. Jamie had promised to copy the photos onto a memory stick for her. The last image on her phone was the one that brought tears to her eyes every time she looked at it. The funeral procession through Wootton Bassett, Royal Wootton Bassett now. The last time their family had been united, following an empty flag-draped box through the crowded streets, the repatriated non-remains of Captain Joshua Mark Steele.

Jamie sensed it was hard for Maddie and Laurel to watch their daughter becoming entranced with a man they'd never known. She hadn't known herself that he'd donated sperm. But there were a lot of things she hadn't known about her brother. She always suspected he was gay but he never talked about his sex life, or lack of it. Whenever her parents questioned him about who he was seeing, he would deflect the topic. Perhaps he thought their mother wouldn't have coped with having two gay children. Or, more likely, focused as he was on his army career, he wouldn't do anything to jeopardise his rise through the ranks.

Josh would, she was sure, have been pleased to know he had a daughter. Maybe it had been in his mind when he joined the army, that if he were killed, he would leave something of himself in the world. Whatever his reasons, they would never know. She had never planned to have children herself, but now she could do something to keep her brother's memory alive and give her newfound niece all the love he would have lavished on her.

Lying in bed staring at the ceiling, she realised that sleep wasn't going to come easily. Finally she reached for her phone and called Van, hoping she was still awake.

Chapter Eight

Phoebe spent a very pleasant few days wandering around the town, along the canal and the river, discovering charming pathways through the woods. The inclement weather had postponed her planned trip onto the moorland, but she was enjoying soaking up the atmosphere of the place. If nothing else, it would provide a great setting for another crime novel.

The small library had a useful section on local history, and she spent many hours perusing their books and maps in the quiet, comfortable surroundings. She also gathered numerous free leaflets from the tourist centre. She perused these avidly, adding to her stock of noteworthy local place names—Dimmin Dale, Top Withins, Fly Flatts, Slack Bottom, Mankinholes, Lumbutts, Jumble Hole.

Friday morning dawned fair, and after a substantial breakfast at one of her newly discovered favourite cafés, she packed her rucksack, donned her walking boots, and set out for the bus stop. She had decided there was no point wearing herself out with a three-mile uphill trek when the bus could drop her off nearer her goal.

Even with the sun shining, the moor stretching out in front of her as she stepped off the bus, looked forbidding. One step at a time she told herself, taking in a lungful of fresh air after the bus had lumbered off, heading down into the next valley. The view was stunning, though. Sheep grazing peacefully, clouds drifting overhead. She took out her phone and snapped a few photos.

The boots started to nip at her ankles as she walked through the first dormant heather stalks near the road. They'd felt fine when she tried them on in the shop. Not too tight, and she was wearing the thick socks recommended by the sales girl. Still, she was sure the circle she was looking for wasn't far away. A few hours at most and she would be back in her comfortable room at the B&B awaiting Sasha's arrival.

After the emotional call the first morning, Sasha had calmed down and she'd been persuaded to come and spend the weekend. Phoebe put Sasha's initial reluctance to join her down to their recent disagreements. But in their conversation the previous night Sasha had shown more enthusiasm and said she was looking forward to it.

Taking another look at the map she was wearing in the plastic holder around her neck, Phoebe thought she was heading the right way. Just a small ridge between her and her goal. A large bird swooped on the air currents overhead. Likely an eagle. She must make a note of that. "Details," Philip had said. "Bring it to life, Phoebe."

†

Things were moving quickly. Jamie had expected the house sale to take the usual five months, but it seemed Mr Corbett was in a hurry to move out. He wanted to be settled in Tewkesbury before Christmas. The estate agent was confident the sale would be completed by the end of the month, only three weeks away. The survey had already been done and there were no structural issues.

She had been round to the house again to take measurements and see what work she would want to do before moving in. Taylor had come with her and offered to help with redecorating. She was full of her visit to the recruiting office. Assuming she would pass their fitness test without any problem, her training programme would start in January.

"Buy a good pair of boots," Jamie advised her.

"Won't they supply all the kit?"

"Yeah. But Josh always said the boots were crap." She offered to take her shopping in Manchester before Christmas to get the boots and a few other things she would need. There was a long list of items she would have to buy for the house, starting from scratch with kitchen appliances, plates, and cutlery. She'd decided it was time to invest in a proper bed as well. The main bedroom in the house was big enough for a queen-size bed.

Friday was another busy day at work. Applications had poured in for the technician jobs and Mike was confident they had a good short list. They would start the interviewing the following week.

Van was coming over that evening and Jamie had promised to take her out for a proper meal to make up for the delayed reunion. Talking to her every evening during the week, Jamie realised how much she wanted to make this relationship work. She couldn't let Sasha take all the blame for their breakup. Despondency over her job had contributed to her partner's decision to look elsewhere. She hadn't been much fun to be with in their final few months together.

†

Waking up to find Phoebe gone and only the briefest of notes on the kitchen table, Sasha had wondered if this was how Jamie had felt. Abandoned. She read through the note twice, disgusted. A bloody writer, she could have made it sound a bit less dismissive.

When she spoke to her later in the day, Phoebe apologised, saying she hadn't realised how it would look to Sasha. She'd been in a hurry. She went on to say how much she was loving this place. And why didn't Sasha join her for the weekend.

Right. A quick look on Google maps confirmed her suspicion. The B&B was only a few streets away from where Jamie lived. Phoebe thought she was still pissed off with her when she'd hesitated. In her subsequent phone calls, her lover went into full seduction mode promising Sasha a night she wouldn't forget.

When Friday came round, Sasha found herself sitting on the train, wondering if she was doing the right thing. There was every chance she would run into Jamie. But if Phoebe lived up to her promise, they would probably spend the entire weekend in bed.

†

It had been a long five days. Van was aching to see Jamie's smile again. Aching to feel those long fingers travel down her body. Sitting still for any length of time all day Friday had been impossible. Connor had commented on the number of loo breaks she'd had before lunchtime.

"Got a bladder problem, Van?"

"Mind your own business, squirt."

"Hey, I'm not the one squirting it out every five minutes."

She threatened to pull his ears but luckily there was a spate of incoming calls and he settled down to work.

Listening to Jamie's voice every night before going to bed wasn't conducive to getting a good night's sleep either. Monday evening when she told her about the revelation that her brother was Taylor's biological father she had sounded emotional. But each night after that, the tone had changed. She was growing into the idea of being an aunt. Taylor was Josh's legacy and now Jamie could be part of nurturing that. She'd shared her thoughts about when or how she was going to tell her parents. Her mother wasn't happy about Jamie's "lifestyle" as she called it, and wouldn't be happy to know that her grandchild had been brought up by two lesbians. Her father, though, would be over the moon to know he had a granddaughter. Van had suggested she tell her dad first and let him break the news to her mother.

Five o'clock finally came round and she shut her computer down with a sigh of relief. Her bag was packed and tucked under her desk, ready for the quick getaway. It would mean fighting her way onto the train and having to stand for most of the journey, but it would be worth it. The sooner she could find herself melting into Jamie's embrace, the better.

✝

The mist descended from nowhere. One minute it was a bright, sunny day, the next she couldn't see past her outstretched hand. The words of the song came into her mind "On Ilkla Moor bar tat," which ended badly for someone she recalled, dying and getting eaten by worms. And all because they were out on the moor without a hat. She had brought a hat.

Phoebe shrugged the backpack off her shoulders and felt around in the main pocket for the nice red woolly hat with a bobble on top. She'd bought it only the day before in one of the local shops, thinking it might come in handy. It wasn't an item of headwear she would normally be seen about in. Hat on, she felt better. No point in dying for the lack of a hat. Now she just had to remember which way it was to the road.

She pulled out her mobile. A compass app would have been useful but her phone didn't have one. Luckily it did have a decent signal strength. *Should bloody well hope so,* she thought. *On top of the fucking moor.*

One message. From Sasha: "I'm on the train." *Damn, I should have been there to meet her.*

"Sash?"

"Where are you?"

"Um, I'm on the moor above the town. I think it's called Oxenhope."

"Right. Are your car keys at the B&B? I can come and get you."

"Well, the problem is, I don't know how to get back to the road."

"What?"

"It's foggy. I can't see a thing."

†

Mike looked up when she arrived back at the office. "Good, I was just going to page you."

"What's up?"

"A woman phoned, Sasha something or other. She wants you to call her back, says its urgent."

"Did she leave her number?"

"Yeah, I wrote it down." He handed her a yellow Post-It note.

She looked at it unsure what to do. A confrontation with her ex wasn't something she wanted to deal with right now.

"She sounded really worried."

"Right. Yeah." Jamie tapped the numbers onto the screen and waited for the connection before holding the phone to her ear. She listened to Sasha's frantic words, asking her to repeat herself. It didn't make sense.

"What's she doing up there?"

"Looking for a stone circle."

"Okay. I'll call it in to Search and Rescue. And I'm on my way as well. Where are you? I'll pick you up."

She looked at Mike after ending the call. "Good thing I brought the car today. Stupid bitch has got herself lost on the moors."

"Who, this Sasha?"

"No. Her girlfriend. Long story." She logged out of her computer and picked up her keys. "Look, I know it's only three o'clock. If anyone asks, I'm at a meeting. Shit, I sound like Jonathan already."

172

Mike laughed. "Just go. I'll be fine. See you Monday."

Driving out of town was going to take a while. There were no quicker routes. Plenty of people leaving early on a Friday, the bypass would be clogged but so would all the other roads leading out of Huddersfield. With the fog getting thicker, more vehicles were coming off the motorway, feeling safer to be crawling along at a snail's pace but adding to the congestion.

Jamie called Andy from the car to explain the situation to him.

"Far as I know, she set off from where the bus stops."

"Right. You'll know it. Remember, we covered that section a few weeks back."

"Okay. But I'm stuck in traffic. I'm not going to get there much before four-thirty. It will be fully dark by then."

"I'll see what I can do about getting a team together. But there have been five call-outs today already. The fog's caught out quite a few ramblers."

Sitting in the queue waiting to get off the bypass and onto the Copley Road, Jamie texted Van.

✝

Huddled into a space next to the luggage rack, she heard her phone ping. A message. She managed to manoeuvre her hands to be able to get it out of her jacket pocket. Message from Jamie. *Emergency. Home later. Code 4218. Spare key on top of door frame. Soz xx.*

She was happy about the "xx" but little else. Looked like it would just be her and Stevie for a while. She settled back into her fantasy of riding a bicycle along the canal towpath, following Jamie, her breath quickening as she imagined holding those gorgeous butt cheeks in her hands again.

✝

Phoebe leant back against the rock and wondered how long she could survive on the meagre ration of a single pack of Kendal Mint Cake. It tasted vile. Why hadn't she brought a Mars bar? She struggled out of her boots and sighed with relief. She couldn't have walked another step with her ankles protesting in agony. She tossed the offending items away. No point dying with her boots on. But she wasn't going to die. She had a hat.

Bloody Philip Pearlman. "Bring it to life," he had said. Ha. Find a stone circle, feel the power. What she needed was power all right. A powerful light.

Closing her eyes, she took several deep breaths. Stay calm. Stay in the zone. She'd read that somewhere. One of the self-help books she sometimes bought, thinking they would help. Help with what? Help being a better lover. Maybe that's why Sasha was running after her ex. What did that computer nerd have that she didn't?

Well, she wasn't lost on top of a fucking moor for a start.

Maybe she could find some wood, start a fire. Oh yeah, she hadn't made it through the first two Brownie sessions without wanting to nut Brown Owl. She was a little light on outdoor skills. She could write, however. Write a light, light a write. Shine a light, had she even remembered to bring a torch? A torch. A flaming piece of wood. With a torch she could set fire to the mist.

What was that bloody poem, one she had to learn in school? Oh yeah, that oft-quoted ode by Keats, "To Autumn." She spoke the first two lines aloud, just wanting to hear her own voice, "Season of mists and mellow fruitfulness, close bosom-friend of the maturing sun..." All she could remember. That and giggling with her best friend over the word *bosom*. They thought *mellow fruitfulness* was pretty funny, too. How old were they? Thirteen.

Survival techniques, books she should have read. It wasn't too late—she could Google it. She poked her phone and the screen lit up. Her connection with the world, the world of safety. No signal. Damn, damn, damn! She was going to die up here after all. Her epitaph could say—at least she wore a hat.

That girl from *Game of Thrones*, Arya. She comforted herself in dire situations by reciting the list of people she wanted to kill. Phoebe started with Philip Pearlman, Jamie Steele, the girl in Year 5 who pushed her over in the playground and stole her ice cream—hell, she'd forgotten her name. Her list of real people was too short. She'd have to resort to the fictional characters she killed off in her crime series.

Maybe it was the mint cake. She was starting to see shapes in the dark. Sheep? No, there it was again, just out of reach. Dancing giants, forming a ring of light.

†

Sasha was pacing up and down outside the B&B when Jamie pulled up. She got in the car, her hands trembling as she buckled the seat belt and Jamie could see that her eyes were red-rimmed from crying. She put her hand on Sasha's leg.

"We'll find her."

"I can't stop thinking the worst. It's hours since she phoned."

"Her battery might have run down, or the signal's crashed. It does that round here."

Jamie had to concentrate on the bit of road she could see in the headlights. Sasha's distress was palpable but Jamie found she wasn't affected by her presence apart from wanting to help find the missing Phoebe. Finding the damn woman and getting back to meet Van were foremost in her thoughts.

As they neared the top of the road leading across the moor, the mist seemed to reach into the car. Even with the fog lights on, it was hard to see anything beyond the beams.

"What is she doing up here, Sasha?"

"It's all my fault."

"How so?"

"I rejected her manuscript." Sasha told her about the science fiction story and Phoebe's determination to see it published. "I'm sure Philip's winding her up to get at me."

Jamie slowed the car to a crawl, not wanting to miss the lay-by next to the bus stop. Her phone rang just as she spotted it and pulled over. It was Andy.

"Bit of a hold up, I'm afraid. Most of the crew is up Rishworth way looking for a group of school kids who were out on a geography field trip. Could be another half hour or more before we can get anyone over to you."

"Okay. I've got my gear in the car. I'll have a scout round."

"Well, try not to get lost yourself."

Jamie reached around behind the passenger seat and pulled out her boots. She opened her door and got out so she could change her footwear.

"I'm coming with you," Sasha said, opening her door.

"No, you're not."

"I can't just sit here."

"There's no point you getting lost as well. If any of the Search and Rescue guys turn up, you'll need to show them where I've started from." She reached into the back of the car and retrieved her coat and her backpack with the fluorescent strips on it. She took the torch out before shouldering the bag.

"I'm leaving the engine running, so the car stays warm, and the headlights on low beam to help show the way back."

Sasha wasn't happy about being left, but going with Jamie really wasn't an option. She wasn't dressed for it.

The light from Jamie's torch only cut through enough mist for her to see where to place her feet on the uneven ground. Sheep droppings were everywhere. Maybe Phoebe had been lucky enough to find a shepherd's shelter. She couldn't recall reading about this situation in the Search and Rescue manual. Probably should have left a trail of breadcrumbs so she could find her way back to the car.

✝

Sasha watched Jamie's form disappear into the fog. Her emotions were all over the place—worry about Phoebe had been foremost until she got into the car and Jamie put a comforting hand on her leg. She had wanted to cover it with her own, keep it there. She wanted to keep Jamie there.

But she had a life with Phoebe now. It was what she thought she had wanted. Was it really only eighteen months ago? A year and a half. Such a short span of time, so many changes.

Jamie had changed as well. She looked grim and determined. Apart from the pat on the knee, there were no lingering looks of affection. Maybe she had someone waiting for her in that attic room. Someone who was willing to share a mattress on the floor with her. Hell, she would, if she got another chance.

Sasha shook herself. No use thinking that way. As her mother would have reminded her, 'she had made her bed, now she had to lie in it.' A lousy homily, she thought, given that it was getting into someone else's bed that had got her into this situation in the first place.

It was getting cold in the car. Would Jamie be able to find Phoebe? Did she care? Of course she did. She wanted her back safe. She would make her feel loved, make herself feel loved. It was all she could do.

†

Suddenly Jamie realised she could see further than the end of the torch beam. The mist was lifting and in a moment it was gone. A cold wind gusted through and swept away the remnants.

She raised the torch and waved it around, calling out Phoebe's name at the same time. After a few moments, she saw it. An answering flash of light off to her right. Five minutes later she was standing over the woman, sitting up calmly with her back resting against a rock.

"Phoebe?" She didn't look at all like the picture on the back of the book. The incongruous red bobble hat hid her hair.

"That's me. I don't think I've had the pleasure." Her words slurred together, sounding like she'd had too much to drink.

"No. We haven't been formally introduced. Jamie Steele."

"Jamie? Sasha's Jamie?"

"Well, not any more, thanks to you." Jamie knelt down next to her. The woman was probably in shock. "Where are your boots?" she asked, noticing Phoebe's feet resting on the grass clad only in brightly coloured socks.

"Oh God, they were killing me. I had to take them off."

Jamie took her phone out and fortunately there was enough signal strength to make a call. "Sasha, I've found her. We're on our way. There's a blanket in the back. We'll need it to warm her up."

She sent a quick text to Andy to let him know before helping Phoebe to her feet. "So, where are your boots?"

"I don't know. I just threw them somewhere."

"Right. Well, we'll take it slow. Just lean on me."

They limped back to the car with Jamie supporting Phoebe as best she could. Sasha was waiting in the back seat with the blanket.

"Take her socks off," Jamie said, throwing her backpack onto the passenger seat. She got behind the wheel and cranked the heat up before setting off.

†

179

Back in the room at the B&B, Sasha plugged in the kettle and made hot chocolate from the sachets provided on the tray while Phoebe stood under a hot shower, moaning with ecstasy. Any other time, Sasha would have been tempted to join her, although she did find sex in the shower hard on the knees these days.

Phoebe came out of the bathroom wrapped in a towel. Another tempting sight.

They sat side by side on the bed sipping the hot chocolate.

"She's kind of cute. Better looking than that picture you have of her."

"Who?"

"Your Jamie."

"She's not my Jamie."

"I can see why you're still lusting after her."

"I'm not."

"So, you buy all your ex-girlfriends expensive sofas. I'll hold out for a three-piece suite at least."

Sasha stared at her. "How did you…?"

"Hm. I have my ways. You've been acting guilty for months now. So, why a sofa? I mean, wouldn't flowers or chocolate be more appropriate if you're trying to woo her."

Sasha looked down at the floor. Time to come clean. "When she came to get Stevie, I drove them back to her place. She's living in this bare attic room. So, yes, I did feel guilty. I had everything and she had nothing."

"Do you want her back?"

"No. Not now."

"But you did. A while ago. That night I was in Wigan. You were with her."

"I wasn't 'with her.' I did track her down. I just wanted to talk."

"About what? About me? What a bitch I am to live with?"

"You're not, and I didn't." Sasha stood and faced Phoebe, placing her hands on her shoulders. "Look, you're still in shock. And so am I. Do you know how frightened I was? I don't want to lose you, Phoebe. Yes, you're a pain in the butt to live with at times. My fault for hooking up with a writer who decides to go off on wild goose chases looking for monoliths. But I do love you."

Phoebe didn't answer right away. When she spoke again, it wasn't the declaration of undying love Sasha hoped to hear.

"I found some stones. We can go back tomorrow and check them out."

"You're not going anywhere. Your feet are a mess. I think we should go to the nearest A&E. Calderdale Royal at Halifax is only a few miles away."

Phoebe pulled away from her, flopping back onto the bed. She covered her eyes with one hand and sighed dramatically. "No way. I'm not spending five hours waiting to see a doctor on a Friday night getting puked on by a bunch of drunks and cokeheads."

"Okay, okay. But I'm taking you home tomorrow and you really should go and see your own doctor on Monday." Sasha carefully lifted Phoebe's unresisting legs onto the bed and covered her with the duvet. By the time she'd finished in the bathroom and crawled in beside her, Phoebe was snoring lightly.

Sasha closed her eyes and tried to calm her own breathing. So much for the night of passion Phoebe had promised. After her encounter with Jamie, Sasha found her thoughts wandering back to the feeling aroused by the pressure of her ex-lover's hand on her leg. How she would have liked it to stay there a bit longer before moving slowly up her thigh. Just thinking of the strength of Jamie's fingers she was getting wet. Using her own hand to satisfy the intense need swiftly coursing through her body, she had to stifle her cries of release so as not to wake her sleeping partner.

✝

Jamie finally found a free parking space further away than she would have liked. She grabbed her trainers and backpack and walked slowly back to her room. It was two hours later than she'd planned to be home that evening. She didn't feel like going out to a restaurant now, she could only hope Van wasn't too disappointed.

She opened the door on a cosy domestic scene. Van was sitting at one end of the sofa reading a magazine with Stevie stretched out next to her. The room smelt of curry and a food carton on the crate was a giveaway. The bottle of wine was mostly empty as well.

"Hi. So sorry. This wasn't the evening I planned." She shrugged out of the wet coat and the backpack, bending down to unlace her boots. Only then did she realise her jeans were wet up to her knees.

"I'm guessing you didn't wear those to work."

"No."

"Oh. I thought, from your message, that it was an emergency at the office."

"Look, I'll hit the shower and then I'll tell you about it. Any wine left?"

When she came back into the main room, she found a glass of wine waiting for her as well as a carton full of curry that looked like it was still hot. She sat down in the space left on the sofa, grateful for both the food and the drink. Stevie had perked up and was staring at her meal with interest.

"I wasn't sure what you liked. It's chicken korma."

"Okay. That's great. How did you manage to keep it warm?"

"I wrapped it in a towel."

Jamie took a mouthful and sighed. "Mm. Thanks. And this is my favourite, by the way."

"So, what happened?"

"Thick fog up on the moors. A woman was stuck up there."

"So, it was a Search and Rescue job?"

"Well, it should have been, but they were all busy finding some school kids." Jamie reached for the wine and took a gulp. She was going to have to tell her. "Um. Sasha phoned. Phoebe, that's her girlfriend, had called her saying she was lost, could Sasha get help."

"So, why didn't she phone the police?"

"I don't know."

Van was looking at the floor. Stevie wormed his way under Jamie's arm and watched her closely as she put food into her mouth. She found a chunk of chicken, licked the sauce off and gave it to him. He snapped it up and leapt off the sofa to enjoy his bounty in privacy.

Jamie got up and retrieved a book from the bookcase. She passed it to Van.

"That's her."

Van looked up again, her eyes not quite meeting Jamie's. "Her?"

"Sasha's girlfriend."

Van turned the book over in her hands. It was the same one she'd picked up the first time she'd visited. "I thought you said her name was Phoebe."

"That's her pen name, Felicity Lemon. Look, I don't know why Sasha called me. But it's a good thing she did. Phoebe could have been stuck there all night before any of the emergency services turned up. As it was, apart from losing her boots, she was in pretty good shape."

"Yeah. Right."

Jamie closed the lid on the carton and moved across to put her arm around Van's shoulders. "Please. I just wanted to be here with you this evening. This week seemed far too long." She brushed the hair from Van's face and moved in for a kiss. Relief surged through her body as Van slowly responded, opening her mouth to let her tongue explore. *Good thing we've both had curry,* was Jamie's last coherent thought as her hand found a breast to caress and Van moaned into her mouth.

†

Lying awake in the middle of the night, it kept going around in her mind. Sasha phoned and Jamie went running. Why couldn't the damn woman have just rung the police? Did Jamie still have feelings for her?

The tears streamed freely, the joy of their lovemaking seeping away, out through her eyes.

Jamie was sleeping soundly, worn out no doubt from saving damsels in distress. But not any old damsel. Her ex-girlfriend's current girlfriend.

She checked the time again on her phone, shielding the glare from the screen with her hand. 5:30. Ten minutes since she'd last looked at it. If she left now it wouldn't be long before the first train.

Methodically, slowly, she extricated herself from the damp sheets. Her clothes were scattered around but she managed to find them and get into the bathroom without waking Jamie. Making as little noise as possible, she peed but didn't flush and decided she would have to wait until she got home before attempting any other ablutions. She had some mints in her bag. They would have to make up for not brushing her teeth.

†

Jamie stirred. She thought she heard the door open and close.

"Van?" Her exploring hand found only empty space next to her.

"Van!" she called, louder this time.

Sitting up, fear gripped her. The room felt strangely empty. Groping around, she found her phone and looked at the time. It was too early for Van to have gone out for coffee. Nothing would be open at this hour. She got up and went into the bathroom. Empty. Turning the light on, she could see that Van's clothes and bag were gone.

She struggled into her clothes. Stevie made himself comfortable in a warm spot in the bed. When her phone beeped she lunged at it. A message: *Sorry. Going home. Don't call.*

What? What had she done? Van couldn't be dumping her like this, by text. It was worse than a note on the kitchen table. But she didn't even have a kitchen, or a table.

Gathering her thoughts she realised that Van hadn't been gone long. If she hurried, she could probably catch her before she got on the train.

At any other time, the run through empty early morning streets would have been exhilarating. But she was too focused on reaching the station quickly. The platform when she reached it was deserted, but looking across to the other side of the track, she could see Van pacing up and down. She raced through the tunnel and up the stairs. A quick glance at the electronic indicator told her the next train was due in two minutes.

"Van!"

Jamie was shocked to see the dark shadows under her eyes. She'd been crying.

"What's wrong? I don't understand. Last night…"

"Last night you were thinking of her."

"I…what…you mean, Sasha…"

"Yes, bloody Sasha. She calls, you run."

Jamie spread her hands, pleading. "She needed help. I'd do the same for anyone."

The train was approaching. Somehow she didn't think this was going to be a soppy *Brief Encounter* moment.

"Jamie, I really like you. But I'm not playing second fiddle to anyone."

"Van, it's not like that. How can you think that?"

The doors of the carriage opened. A passenger got out and Van stepped in. Jamie made to follow her, but Van placed a hand on her chest and pushed her away.

"No. Right now, this hurts. Just leave me alone."

Jamie stood helplessly, watching the train pull away, watching until it disappeared around the bend. She sat down on a bench, head in hands. She didn't know how long she'd sat there before a voice above her said, "You all right, son?"

She didn't disabuse the well-meaning stranger of his mistake. Just kept her head down. "Yeah, fine thanks."

More people were arriving. Saturday workers. It was too early for the shopping crowd. After another train had come and gone, she got up and walked slowly back to her room. Stevie greeted her with the plaintive meows that meant he wanted feeding. After filling his bowl, Jamie lay on the mattress and gave in to the tears that she could no longer hold back.

✝

Sasha woke up in a strange bed and stretched to find the space beside her empty. She lay still listening to the sounds of the world outside coming to life. Traffic moving along the road, birds tweeting, a toilet flushing in the next room. Finally, sitting up, she saw Phoebe seated at the dressing table scribbling on a notepad.

"Morning."

Phoebe carried on writing. Sasha watched her noting, as the morning sun filtered through the curtains highlighting the writer's head, that the dark roots were showing. Time for another trip to her hairdresser. Probably higher on her "to do" list than visiting the doctor to have her feet examined.

Phoebe stopped writing and glanced towards the bed. "Oh, good. You're awake. I composed a poem, you know. Up on the moor when the mist came down. I just needed to get it down while I remembered the words. Do you want to hear it?"

Sasha didn't have the heart to say no. "Yes."

"I think it will be the centrepiece for *The Moons of Septimus Seven*." With an intake of breath, Phoebe launched into her best reading voice for the recital.

"Water covers the King's lands,
And three moons circle the globe.
Send home the great rings of Light
By the music of the Spheres.
In setting fire to the night
Balance will be restored
To a thousand years of Space."

When she finished, Phoebe sat back in the chair and beamed at Sasha, "Isn't that great? I think Philip will love it."

I think Philip's a dick and you should go back to crime. Sasha breathed out, slowly, thankful for the still dark room so Phoebe couldn't see her expression. "That's wonderful, honey."

Phoebe didn't seem to hear the lack of enthusiasm in her tone.

"Honestly, Sash. I did see something just before the mist came down. A standing stone, more than one, it could have been my circle."

"I don't care if it was a full-sized henge with druids dancing round it, you're not going back up there."

Phoebe shifted in the chair. "But…"

"No buts. I'm taking you home. First, though, I'll call Jamie to thank her. I was too concerned about getting you inside last night and she shot off before I could say anything."

"You have her phone number?" Phoebe's accusing tone hit a high note.

"Yes."

Phoebe pulled away from her. "And you expect me to believe it's all over."

"I rang her at work, that's the only number I had for her. But she called me back on her mobile, so I saved the number in case I needed it. I was worried sick about you, Feebs."

"Send her a text."

"I can't thank her for saving your life by text. I'll call her in a bit."

Sasha waited for another outburst, but it didn't come. Phoebe just got up and hobbled into the bathroom. After flushing the toilet she stood in the doorway and said, "A thousand years of space. Do you think that's a better title than *The Moons of Septimus Seven*?"

"No. It sounds like a science manual."

"Oh." Phoebe moved away from her and leant over the edge of the bed.

Sasha could hear her rummaging through their tangle of clothes on the floor. What now? She wasn't planning on reading more of her manuscript to her, was she? As if having years taken off her life by worrying about her being lost on the moor wasn't punishment enough. It was a relief when Phoebe simply handed over her phone.

"She must be up by now. Didn't strike me as someone who lies about in bed half the morning. So, ring her."

"Ring her?"

"Your girlfriend. You know, the skinny one with the cat and the sofa."

"Phoebe!"

"Go on. Ring her now. But I'll be listening."

Sasha poked at the phone and found the number. The call didn't last long. Jamie sounded distant, not really interested. Perhaps she'd woken her up.

"Satisfied?" Sasha asked, ending the call.

"Not really. I could murder a coffee though. There's a great café in the square and it will be open by now."

"Are you sure you want to walk anywhere? They do breakfast here."

"I know. But it's a bit boring. Much more fun to do some people watching while we eat." She sat back down at the dressing table and started to brush her hair.

Sasha realised there was no point arguing. By the time she came out of the bathroom, Phoebe was fully dressed and itching to go.

"Come on, Sash, I'm starving."

And so was she, Sasha realised. Their only sustenance the night before had been hot chocolate and a stale biscuit.

The short walk to the café was painfully slow and Phoebe had to lean on Sasha, stopping every few yards.

"Are you sure you want to do this? We can just pack up now and go home?"

"No, no. You'll love this place. Honestly, Sasha, I think I could live here."

Sasha laughed. "Don't be ridiculous. It's fine for a holiday. But you'd be bored out of your mind in no time." "Well, maybe a holiday flat, then. The atmosphere is so, I don't know, it's just so relaxed. I know I could write here."

Was that really the problem, Sasha wondered, as they finally arrived at the café? Did Phoebe have writer's block? Well, whatever it was, the sooner they got back to civilisation the better as far as she was concerned. She certainly couldn't live in a place with Jamie in close proximity.

Sasha pushed the guilty thought of her nighttime activity to the back of her mind and seeing Phoebe safely seated went to the counter to order their coffee leaving her to peruse the menu. Breakfast, then home, back to normality. In a few days, Phoebe would have moved on to something else.

Chapter Nine

The shopping expedition had been a success. Jamie was stocking up on supplies for her new kitchen. She needed everything—plates, glasses, and cutlery—a new start for the new house.

Taylor was standing by a mirror looking down at her feet in the glass. "These boots are ace." She had insisted on wearing them out of the shop.

"If they start to hurt, take them off. No point getting blisters."

"Yes ma'am."

"Stop it."

"Just practicing."

They walked on through the housewares department.

"Time for a coffee break before we head back to the car with this stuff."

"Okay. Coffee shop is on the fourth floor."

They were able to get a table after a family of four had vacated it. Taylor cleared the debris left behind onto a tray and parked it in the shelving left for that purpose.

"You think they could teach their kids some manners," she said when she returned to the table.

"Too busy looking at their phones, all four of them. So, what do you want? I'm having a cappuccino."

Taylor eventually decided on a mocha latte with a cranberry and custard muffin.

"Annie's keen to come and help with the painting tomorrow. Is that okay?"

"Assuming you've already told her it is, yes."

They talked about the jobs that needed doing in the house. It was starting to come together. The bed had been delivered the day before along with the kitchen appliances. Taylor had helped her out by staying in for the deliveries while Jamie was at work. As a reward, Jamie had brought her into Manchester to buy the army boots.

"It'll be nice to have a washing machine again. That laundromat's the pits. Nothing ever really felt clean."

"I should think it's nice to have a kitchen, period. I don't know how you stuck it in that dump for so long."

"I hear your mother talking there."

"Get lost."

Jamie smiled at the youngster. Spending time with Taylor over the last few weeks had helped her get through some of the lonely evenings since Van's abrupt departure from her life. The girl wanted to know all about Josh and Jamie found it wasn't so painful sharing the memories of her brother. She had spoken to her dad and he'd been delighted to know he had a granddaughter. He and Veronique, his young wife, had already booked a Christmas holiday, but he

193

told Jamie he would definitely make plans to come over sometime in the following year.

"Have you made your choices for what you want to do in the army?"

"Yes. There are a lot of options, but eventually I want to drive tanks."

Jamie almost choked on the froth she had just spooned into her mouth. "That's a bit frontline. Couldn't you do something like communications? I'll bet your parents aren't thrilled. That'll put you right into the danger zones."

"Riding a bike is dangerous. I'll bet more people are killed here cycling than have died in a tank."

Jamie bit back a retort and spooned out the last bit of chocolate-covered froth from the bottom of the cup.

"Hey, isn't that Van? She's with some bloke, looks about twelve."

Jamie turned her head. It was Van. The young man with her was probably Connor, the lad she worked with. "Be right back," she said, getting up quickly.

They were standing in front of a glassware display. She walked up behind Van. "Hi."

Van jumped, almost knocking over a row of long stemmed wine glasses.

"Just doing some shopping. Things for the house. Moved in yesterday." Jamie turned to Connor. "Could you give us a few moments, please?"

Connor nodded and moved away. Van took a step as if to follow him. Jamie put a hand on her arm.

"Please. Hear me out. I can't stop thinking about you. I know we only had a few nights together but I've missed you. I liked waking up with you there. I want to make it work."

The slate blue eyes were unreadable. Jamie didn't know what to do. She wanted to press her against the cabinet and kiss her.

Finally Van said, "I'll think about it." She walked away and Jamie's eyes followed her all the way across the room until she disappeared from view with young Connor trailing after her.

†

Connor waited until they were on the escalator going down to the next level before saying, "Wow! Is she the one who's got your knickers in a twist?"

Van didn't respond. She was still in shock. Seeing Jamie just brought back the last image she'd had of her, the one that had haunted her dreams every night for the past two weeks—standing forlornly on the station platform, hair sticking out at all angles, face flushed from running.

Steering her into the Spanish restaurant they'd agreed on earlier, Connor ordered a bottled beer for both of them once they were seated.

"It's not over, is it?"

"It's never over until the fat lady sings. I guess that's me. Only I don't feel much like singing."

"You're not fat. Just well filled out in places. Anyway, the way she looked at you, I wish someone would look at me like that."

"Like what?"

"Like if you weren't standing in the middle of a posh department store, she would have fucked you then and there."

"You're full of shit, as usual."

"No, really."

"Can we change the subject? What did you think of those wine glasses we were looking at before we were interrupted? Do you think they're okay for my cousin's wedding present?" Van picked up the menu without waiting for his answer.

They ordered half a dozen tapas dishes to share but Connor ate most of them. Van picked at things listlessly, her mind not fixated on food for once.

†

Sasha was hoping things would return to normal soon, or what counted for normal in her life with Phoebe. The writer had worked feverishly for two days revising *The Moons of Septimus Seven* before sending the manuscript back to Philip Pearlman. Sasha figured he would wait a few weeks before sending her a final rejection letter. She was ready for that eventuality and had booked a Christmas holiday in the Maldives.

Phoebe had been distant of late, though, not initiating any sexual contact. Since the return from her adventure on the moor, she had just turned over in bed each evening saying she was tired. Sasha had experienced this before and figured she was incubating ideas for her next novel. The dry spell never lasted long.

Returning home from a long day of meetings and looking forward to dinner with friends, Sasha only hoped there wouldn't be any drama when she got home. The day before she had been greeted with the sight of Phoebe struggling with a large object by the front door.

"What's that?"

"What does it look like?" Phoebe stood back, hands on hips. "Your nutty ex has sent the sodding sofa back. The delivery prick just left it here. Wouldn't even shift it into the garage for me."

Sasha looked at the sofa with dismay. That was all she needed now. More angst about whether or not she was still in love with Jamie. Noting the mutinous look on Phoebe's face, she quickly said, "I'll ask Nick next to door to help move it."

"It's your problem, Sash." Phoebe walked back into the house and Sasha thought she heard her add, "It always has been."

That was yesterday. This evening things could be looking up. Checking the clock on the dashboard as she pulled into the drive, she figured on time enough for a quick drink before needing to get showered and changed. It was only a short taxi ride to Cynthia's place in Heywood. Hoping that going out together would break her partner's bad mood; she let herself into the house to see Phoebe carrying a heavy-looking box down the stairs. She set it down and looked up at Sasha, red-faced.

"What's that? Do you need help with it?"

"Just some books for my reading next week." Phoebe sat on the bottom step looking close to tears.

"Okay. You look done in. I'll take this out to your car and then bring you a drink."

"Thanks. Just water though."

Sasha took Phoebe's car keys off the hall table and picked up the box.

"Put it on the back seat, please. It's easier for me to lift out."

"Okay, sweetheart."

197

Returning to the kitchen after depositing the box in the car, Sasha prepared a gin and tonic for herself and wondered if Phoebe was coming down with something. Maybe that was contributing to her shitty mood lately. She carried the glasses through to the living room and set the water down on the table. Phoebe was lying on the sofa with a hand over her eyes.

"Are you okay?"

"Just a bit tired."

"What have you been doing today?" Sasha thought Phoebe had been working on a new story idea. She'd been ensconced in her office when she left for work that morning.

"Shopping."

There hadn't been any evidence in the hallway. Not the usual array of department store bags which indicated a boost to the UK's GDP.

"Didn't see anything you liked?"

"My feet hurt so I came home."

Sasha sipped her drink. "Are you still okay to go out this evening?"

"Were we going out this evening?"

Another sickness symptom, Phoebe was usually champing at the bit to go places, a chance to show off a recently purchased designer outfit.

"Yes. Dinner with Cynthia and the rest of the crowd." They were her friends, but she thought Phoebe generally enjoyed the times they'd met up.

A heavy sigh. Phoebe dropped her arm but her eyes stayed closed. "I don't really feel up to it. You go."

"I'll stay home if you're not well."

"No, I'd feel guilty if you didn't go."

"Well, if you're sure. I haven't seen Cyn for a while."

"Yes, you go. I'll be okay here."

"Do you want me to bring you back something to eat?"

"No, I don't really feel like anything."

"I feel bad, leaving you like this."

"It's okay. I'd rather you went. I won't be good company."

Sasha finished her drink and stood. "I'd better get ready, then."

She had reached the door when Phoebe called out, "Oh, don't mind the mess in the bedroom. I was just doing some sorting out. I'll clear it up in a bit."

The bedroom was certainly in disarray, not as she'd left it that morning. Clothes everywhere, two big suitcases open on the floor. It was another month before their trip to the Maldives but perhaps Phoebe had been trying on outfits. Whenever they went anywhere, even if it was only overnight, she would spend days deciding which clothes to take, often deciding she didn't have anything to wear. Which then necessitated another shopping trip to Selfridges or Harvey Nicks.

Sasha sat on the bed and fingered the flimsy material of the black cocktail dress closest to her. She hadn't seen this one before. Life with Jamie had been so much simpler, she thought. Her ex-girlfriend's idea of dressing up consisted of a clean pair of jeans and a tailored shirt, likely one that Sasha had bought to enhance Jamie's limited wardrobe.

Showered and changed, Sasha went into the living room to say goodbye. Phoebe had rolled over on her side, but Sasha was sure she wasn't really asleep. The sound of a horn outside alerted her to the arrival of her taxi. She kissed Phoebe's head and stroked her arm. "Catch you later, babe. I won't be late."

She thought she heard a muttered "Have fun," as she left the room. Sitting in the back of the taxi, Sasha smiled to herself. The evening out would do her good and in the morning she would talk to Phoebe, find out what was going on.

✝

Laurel dabbed at her eyes. "She's too young. I can't believe they let kids join up at sixteen in this country. They're always banging on about child soldiers in other places."

"She won't be sent to any trouble spots before she's eighteen." Maddie held onto Laurel, feeling her body trembling. She had the same fears for their daughter, but the changes she'd seen in Taylor in the last few weeks were so positive she didn't want to let them show. The moody teen was gone. She was blossoming into a young woman before their eyes. But in a few weeks she would be gone, off to her training camp. When they next saw her, she would have changed even more.

"It's just, I feel like she's been taken from us already. She's spending all this time with Jamie. And now knows she has a new grandfather who wants to meet her."

"Well, we have to make the most of this time we have with her. Leo will be home for Christmas. We'll all be together as a family. This is what she wants to do, love. We have to let her know we support her, and that we're always here for her. I suspect she needs that more than ever now. She's taking a big step and probably doesn't even realise yet just how big a step it is."

"It's so sudden. I'm not ready to let her go so soon. Right after Leo. I thought we'd have a good few years before she left the nest."

Maddie held her and let her cry. It was all she could do.

†

They were half-way home before Taylor tentatively asked, "So, what did she say?"

Jamie kept her eyes on the road, checking the rearview mirror before changing lanes. "She said she'd think about it."

"Oh."

Thankfully Tay decided not to pursue the subject and sat quietly for the rest of the journey fiddling with her phone. Once they had unloaded the car, Jamie talked Taylor through the plans for the next day.

"I'll have to leave you in charge of the painting in the front room. You can make as much mess as you like. I haven't taken the wrappings off the new suite yet. You'll need to cover the floor though. I have to live with that carpet until the fitters come at the end of next week."

"What are you going to be doing?"

"The bathroom needs a good going over. Then I'll be plumbing in the washing machine. And then I'll start on the hallway. Are you sure Annie's okay with helping out? It is a Sunday and looks like being a nice day."

"Sure. She's cool about it."

Sipping tea from one of the new mugs, Jamie raised an eyebrow. She put the mug down on the counter. "Must be a special friend if she wants to come and slave here all day."

"It's not like that. We've been friends like forever."

"Right. If you say so. I'll expect you here about ten. Okay?"

"Yes, ma'am!" Taylor snapped to attention with a salute.

"Not bad. But make sure your feet are together. Have you been keeping up with the running?"

"Yep. Every day."

Passing the army medical had been easy for Tay, but Jamie told her the exercise regime once she started training would be much tougher than any of her school PE classes. Luckily the girl had taken her advice onboard with enthusiasm and had started a programme of running and lifting weights.

"See you tomorrow." Tay flashed her a big smile, gave her a quick hug, and was gone.

Her smile, so much like Josh's. Jamie wondered how she had never noticed it before. But, of course, she hadn't been looking for it.

Alone with her thoughts for the evening, Jamie sat on a stool in the kitchen. Her first cooking venture was heating up soup in the microwave. The old man's stove was the one appliance she hadn't bothered replacing. It was in good condition, and didn't look like it had been used much. Taylor had removed all the packaging and wiped down the fridge when it was delivered, so all Jamie had to do was plug it in when she got back. She had done her first big grocery shop on the way home, having promised to supply beer and pizza for her two helpers.

Stevie had gone out into the garden to explore his new territory after a few comic moments spent mastering the cat flap in the back door. His head poked through now just as the oven pinged to let her know the soup was done.

"It's minestrone, buddy. You won't like it."

He pulled the rest of his body through the opening and looked up at her as if to say, "Try me."

She carried the bowl into the front room and he followed her. The tins of paint, brushes and trays were lined up ready for the morning. She perched on the edge of the new recliner and surveyed her domain. It felt good to have somewhere that would eventually look like a home.

Tay had asked when she was getting a television. It wasn't high on her list of priorities. However, she would be getting a new desktop computer. She had been staying late at the office the last few weeks to finish up admin jobs that needed doing, but a lot of them could have been done at home. The smallest bedroom she would turn into an office, leaving the third one to be used as a guest room. Not that she expected to have many visitors. If her father and Veronique did visit, they could have her bed.

Keeping busy during the day with her new responsibilities at work and the finalising of the house sale, she managed to banish intruding thoughts of Van. The nights weren't so easy, though. She would get a few hours sleep at most. The rest of the time was spent tossing and turning, torturing herself with images of Van's warm body, responsive lips on hers. Her mind refused to let it go despite telling herself over and over that she wasn't in love with Van, she'd only known her a few weeks. They'd slept together, what, four times. That hardly signified the start of a deep and lasting relationship. But no matter how she rationalised it during the day, at night her emotions took over and her body shook with a longing that couldn't be satisfied.

†

She always enjoyed Cynthia's dinner parties. The food was excellent with accompanying wine that rivalled any top restaurant selections. Sasha loved the time spent with her oldest friends and she expected this evening to be no different. Phoebe's absence wasn't unwelcome, it gave her the chance to interact more naturally with the others.

They had finished their main course and Cynthia asked if Sasha could help her in the kitchen.

"Everything okay?" she asked when the door had closed, shutting them off from the dining room.

"Sure." Sasha placed the plates she'd collected on the counter.

"You know, we were all a bit surprised when you dumped Jamie."

"What? None of you ever had a good word to say about her."

"Oh, you can be a bit thick sometimes, Sash. Everyone here had a massive crush on her. She was so adorably cute. Who can resist the dark, silent type? And that awesome butt of hers, I was constantly wiping drool off the sofa every time she bent down." Cynthia had spent six months in New York and now her normally flawless Oxbridge educated English was peppered with words like 'cute' and 'awesome'.

"So why were you lot always saying she wasn't good enough for me?"

"You are dim. Lorna was definitely hoping for a chance with her when you left. Only she hadn't counted on Jamie being so broken up about your defection."

Sasha held onto the counter.

"Anyway, what's Phoebe's excuse for not coming tonight?" Cynthia started taking the pre-prepared desserts out of the fridge.

"I told you. She's not feeling well. When I checked on her before I left, she'd fallen asleep on the sofa."

"Hm. Drinking at lunchtime can do that to you."

"She said she was shopping."

"Well, if that's what she calls it. I'm sorry, Sasha, but she and her dining companion were heading for the hotel lifts hand in hand after they finished the last of the wine."

Sasha felt as if she'd been punched in the stomach. "Which hotel?"

"The Radisson Blu. I was there with a client."

Cynthia closed the distance between them and held her. Sasha was shaking.

"I'm so sorry, hon. I wouldn't have told you, but it's not the first time I've seen her there in recent months with the same woman."

The numbness stole over her as Cynthia guided her to a chair. She was only vaguely aware of her friend telling her to sit there as long she wanted. She heard Cynthia moving about, taking the desserts, voices drifting in from the dining room. How could she ever face them, or anyone, again?

The shock wore off gradually and she gulped down the glass of brandy Cynthia had left for her on the kitchen table. The suitcases, the clothes on the bed. It dawned on her slowly, Phoebe was leaving her. She'd even helped by putting that box in the car. *What an idiot!* She moved slowly, her legs still wobbly, to the phone on the wall. Dialling home the answer phone picked up after six rings and she heard Phoebe's cheerfully recorded words: 'We're not here. Leave a message after the tone and we'll get back to you, if we want to talk to you.'

She put the receiver back in its cradle and slumped back into the chair, head in her hands. This couldn't be happening, not to her, not now.

†

Sunday dawned bright and clear, a perfect autumn day with just the hint of oncoming winter chill. Jamie crawled out of bed exhausted from her restless night. She ran through the list of chores in her head and decided a bike ride would help get her motivated.

Taking the road out of town towards Haworth, the steep uphill climb with its twists and turns quickly had her legs and heart pumping. Reaching the top, the beauty of the early morning sun's rays hitting the bare moorland, with the patchwork quilt of stone-walled fields in the foreground, gave Jamie the balm she needed to settle her restless mind.

The exhilarating run back down the hill into town was the final boost to her system that she needed to kick-start her day.

Stevie was waiting in the kitchen so she put out his food and replenished his water bowl before heading upstairs for a shower. She had used some of her pent-up frustration the evening before by scouring the bathroom, so that was one task out of the way. Sometime in the near future she would need to give it a proper makeover, but it was serviceable for now with a decent water pressure flow from the taps— surprising given the age of the property. She would probably have a major plumbing job on her hands if there were, as she suspected, mainly lead piping under the floorboards. Best to get the professionals in for that job.

Sitting on the new plastic-wrapped sofa in the front room with her coffee and toast, a contented Stevie on her lap, Jamie thought she had a lot to be thankful for—she was healthy, enjoyed her work, and now owned a house and a car. There was no point pining over what might have been with Van. The work that needed doing in the house would keep her occupied at least until Christmas.

She really didn't want to think about Christmas and her fast approaching fiftieth birthday. No doubt Maddie and Laurel would invite her to spend the day with them, but she might just tell them she was going to Spain and hide out in her new home instead.

A knock on the door startled her and moments later Taylor barged in, followed by her friend, Annie.

"Hey, you're early," Jamie said, getting to her feet and placing Stevie on the sofa.

"Yeah. Well, we can't wait to get started. Right, Annie?"

The other girl just looked up at her friend and smiled. She seemed rather sweet and shy. If Jamie didn't know she was the same age as Taylor, she would have thought she was about fourteen.

"Help yourselves to coffee, or there's tea if you prefer. You know where everything is, Tay. I'll just get the lids off the paint cans and get you started."

Jamie smiled as she heard them clattering about the kitchen, a sudden burst of laughter from Tay. Just what the house needed, a bit of life as well as a facelift. She opened the tins, unwrapped the trays and roller brushes, and waited for her two helpers to return.

†

Van remembered the street, but not the house number. Then she saw the black cat seated in a front window. Stevie. He seemed to be watching her. Clutching the potted plant she'd picked up at the florist on her way through the town from the station, she walked up the path to the front door.

It was ajar; she could hear a song she didn't recognise blaring out. Pushing the door open she walked into a scene of chaos. Dust sheets everywhere. Taylor, her blonde hair hidden under a baseball cap was standing on top of a ladder stretching to reach a corner near the ceiling with a paint-laden brush. Another girl was holding the ladder and laughing at something Tay had said. She turned and noticed Van.

"Hi." She had to shout over the music. "Is Jamie here?"

"Yeah. In the kitchen. Through there."

Stevie had jumped off the window ledge and was looking up at her. He meowed once, and then walked off in the direction Taylor had indicated. Van followed, narrowly avoiding stepping on a paint tray.

The legs sticking out from under the sink were the only indication of human presence—a vision of muscular calves and thighs clad only in black boxer shorts. Stevie gave one of the legs a lick before disappearing through the cat flap.

Van feasted her eyes on the exposed flesh in front of her before gathering her wits enough to announce her presence by saying, "Nice view!"

The rest of Jamie's body slid out and she looked up from the floor. Van had to close her mouth so as not to embarrass herself by drooling. The shorts and a tight-fitting t-shirt were the only bits of clothing Jamie was wearing. Seeing Van she leapt to her feet, just managing to miss hitting her head on the underside of the cupboard.

Van held out the plant. "This is a housewarming present. I wasn't sure what you needed."

"Well, the plant's great. I don't need another toaster." Their hands touched as Jamie took the plant from her and when she moved away to place it on the counter, Van felt the loss of contact keenly.

Looking into Jamie's brown eyes when she turned back round, Van wondered how she could ever have doubted her. Her lower lip trembled. She didn't know how to start saying she was sorry for the way she'd acted.

Jamie saved her from having to say anything by pulling her close and kissing her. The kiss seemed to last forever, and Van wanted it to, but eventually they had to break apart to take in air. Jamie caressed her face gently.

"I've missed you so much."

"I'm an idiot. Can you forgive me?"

"I already have."

They kissed again.

A stifled giggle from the doorway brought them out of another trancelike state. Without turning around, Jamie said, "The pizza boxes are on the counter, beer's in the fridge. Help yourselves and bugger off."

"They're underage," Van protested after the girls had disappeared with their booty.

"Preparing Tay for army life. She needs to be able to hold her own with the boys." Jamie grinned down at her. "Would you like to see the bedroom?"

"Does it have a bed in it?"

"Queen size, box spring, headboard. Just needs road testing."

"In that case, the answer is yes."

Jamie took her by the hand and led her upstairs.

✝

The bedroom walls were still covered in the hideous floral design wallpaper that Jamie was sure had gone out of fashion in the middle of the last century. It was next on her list of things to do. Stripping it down to the bare plaster would be a pleasure. But right now the only stripping to be done was taking the clothes off the woman in front of her.

Van was smiling as she glanced around. "Still some work to be done here, I see."

"Yes. Best to just close your eyes."

When Van complied, Jamie took her time, starting with soft kisses on her eyelids. She moved her hands slowly down, unbuttoning the blouse while she placed more tender kisses on Van's neck. The bra was a front fastener giving easy access to the plump, full breasts she knew she would find there, nipples already hardening.

Her own body was responding rapidly to the sensation of skin on skin, and breathing in the scent of the other woman's arousal, as she unzipped her jeans and placed a hand on panties already soaked through.

"Mm. I guess you're ready for this."

"I've dreamed of nothing else for two weeks." Van squirmed as Jamie's fingers found their way under the knicker elastic.

"Me too."

"Please, Jamie. I want you now."

Deciding that slow and easy wasn't going to work for either of them, Jamie pushed Van onto the bed and swiftly removed shoes, jeans, panties, and her own boxer shorts. Finally able to taste the woman she'd desperately wanted during those long, lonely nights, she didn't hold back and used her tongue to bring Van to the edge of orgasm. When Van grabbed her hair and screamed her name, she pushed three fingers inside and was rewarded with an almost instant flow of juices into her mouth. Pulling herself up to meet Van's lips with a sloppy, wet kiss, she paused long enough to say, "That was just for starters."

Van moved her hips provocatively under her and grabbed her butt with both hands. "Good."

Jamie took a deep breath and took the slower route this time, kissing Van's neck while caressing each breast in turn before giving the fully erect nipples her attention. She could feel Van's wetness on the thigh now trapped between her lover's legs and the increased rubbing motion was bringing Jamie to the edge of a much needed climax.

Several orgasms later, exhausted, they were both fading into sleep. Jamie whispered, "Promise me you'll be here when I wake."

The answer was a gentle snore.

✝

They sat side by side on the cloth-draped couch. Annie licked the last of the tomato off her fingers and looked over at Taylor. She'd taken her cap off and her newly shorn blonde hair was sticking up at different angles. Annie reached out to smooth a few strands down.

"I like it like this."

"Yeah. Mum went ballistic. But I told her it would grow. And I like it. Wish I'd cut it years ago."

"You know, that Shaz is an idiot."

"Oh?" Tay gave her friend a quizzical look.

"I wouldn't have minded if you'd kissed me."

"You wouldn't?"

Annie looked into her eyes and wondered if she'd said too much. They had been best friends since their first day at nursery school. She glanced away.

"Annie. I didn't know you felt like that."

"No, well, you were too busy trying to impress someone else."

Taylor grabbed her hand. "Do you still want to…kiss me?"

"I suppose." Annie found her gaze fixated on her friend's full lips. She ran her tongue around her own.

Taylor leaned in and found her mouth, using one hand to pull her head closer. The softness and warmth engulfed her. Kissing her best friend was everything and more than she had dreamed of; Annie wanted to stay in Taylor's embrace forever.

†

The black cat surveyed the two bodies now entwined on his favourite resting place. Humans! He poked a paw at the empty pizza box. Not a scrap left. He wandered through to the feeding room. No Jayjay, no food. Strolling over to the door he poked his head through the flap. Hm. A world to explore. He pushed through and sat on the step. Birds in the trees. He set off down the grassy space, tail twitching. A present for Jayjay.

Yes. This was the life.

✝

Waking up in the bed and finding Van still asleep beside her, Jamie felt an overwhelming sense of contentment. She checked the time. It was three o'clock. The house was quiet. Too quiet. She remembered the girls who were painting in the front room. No music. Had they bunked off early seeing as Jamie was otherwise occupied and not likely to check up on them?

Gently extricating herself from Van's embrace, she pulled on her shorts, grabbed a t-shirt from the closet and crept downstairs. She thought the room was empty at first before catching sight of the two bodies in close proximity on the couch. So the bed wasn't the only new piece of furniture being christened. *Well, well, Taylor and Annie, who knew?* She was sure Tay hadn't known until today.

She moved quietly into the kitchen and closed the door. There were two beers left in the fridge. She uncapped them and prepared a plate of cheese and crackers to take upstairs. A light snack to see them through to the evening. Tonight she really would take Van out for a proper meal.

A loud meow disturbed her thoughts. She turned to see Stevie backing through the cat flap. He was having difficulty getting his head through. With one last effort he managed it, falling back onto the floor. She wanted to laugh but then saw what he had dropped. He looked up at her, waiting for her approval. A dead bird. He pushed it towards her with one paw and meowed again.

"Oh, Stevie. It's for me? That's sweet of you." She squatted down and patted his head, scratching lightly behind his ears. Green eyes stared searchingly into hers. She'd read somewhere that looking cats directly in the eyes was seen by them as an act of aggression. Stevie never minded though. Right now he was looking for her approval and she didn't want to upset him by refusing his gift.

"I'll save it for later. But thank you."

There was a roll of paper towel on the counter. She tore off a few sheets to pick up the bird carefully and place it on the counter by the door. Stevie seemed happy with this and after wrapping his body through her legs a few times, disappeared out the cat flap. She watched him stroll across the yard. He already had a favourite perch on the low wall at the back. Finding the plastic bags she'd stashed in a cupboard, she slipped the bird inside one of them and put the package in the bin.

She washed her hands at the kitchen sink before heading back upstairs. The two girls were still engaged in an intimate embrace and didn't see her pass through.

✝

Van opened her eyes to see Jamie entering the room clutching two bottles of beer in one hand, carrying a plate in the other.

"Thought you might be hungry. I know I am," she said, setting the plate on the bed.

"Aren't you worried about getting crumbs everywhere?"

"Not really." She grinned at her. "I think the sheets might need changing after today's activity anyway."

Struggling to sit up, Van clutched the duvet to her exposed breasts. Jamie put the beers down and slipped off the boxers to rejoin her under the cover. She passed over a bottle.

"It seems the kids downstairs have also discovered the delights of afternoon sex. I hope Laurel's not going to come after me for corrupting her daughter."

Van took a sip of her beer. "She'll probably be relieved it's finally happened. They were talking about it last time I was there. Laurel had only just picked up on Tay's potential baby-dykeness."

"Yeah, well, it seems the girl's spent most of her teenage years trying to fit in with the beauty queens at school. It's been good to see her finding out she can be herself and the world's not going to end."

"Guess she's had her auntie Jamie to thank for that."

"I don't know that I'm a fit role model."

Van leant in and kissed her. "You're fit enough." Her tummy rumbled loudly. Jamie laughed and passed her a cracker.

"This is just to keep starvation at bay. You can decide where I'm taking you for dinner."

Van chewed the cracker slowly, savouring the flavour of the mature cheddar cheese. "Mmm," she said, once she'd swallowed. "Can't we just stay here?"

"Well the kids have eaten all the pizza and Stevie's brought me a dead bird, so I think eating out is the best option."

215

Van drank some more beer and looked into Jamie's serious brown eyes. "Okay. If you can promise me that your demented ex isn't going to show up, I wouldn't mind going back to the wine bar. I seem to remember the food was pretty good, before we were rudely interrupted."

Jamie smiled. "Great. Let's start storing up good memories."

Van's heart lurched. That sounded like a commitment of sorts. She placed her hand on Jamie's chest, above her heart. "If you remove your t-shirt, I think we can add to the bank of good memories already started."

Epilogue

A fine June day and the families milled about in the sunshine waiting for the newly qualified soldiers to be released from the parade ground at the end of their Passing Out ceremony.

Robert Steele put his arm around Laurel's shoulders. "You've done a fine job with her, my dear. I can't believe how much she looks like our Josh, especially in uniform." He'd spent the evening before saying much the same thing again and again as he pored over the pictures of Taylor. Maddie and Laurel had taken him through all the stages of Taylor's life to date, starting with the early baby photos.

Jamie spotted her niece first, weaving her way through the crowd. She waved to her and Taylor reached them in a few confident strides. She hugged her parents and Leo first, and stood back to be introduced to the only other male in their group. Jamie did the honours.

"Tay, meet your grandfather, Robert." They had agreed between them that he didn't want to be called "grandpa" or any other form of grandparent type address.

217

"Pleased to meet you, Private Hope. Congratulations."

They shook hands formally, but Jamie knew it wouldn't be long before they were in each other's arms. Her father's time in Spain with his younger lover had made him more demonstrative than he'd ever been while she was growing up.

"Sorry my wife couldn't be here. She very much wants to meet you."

Jamie bit her lip. He wasn't talking about her mother. In the brief conversation he'd had with his ex wife to let her know she had a granddaughter, she'd cut him short. "She doesn't want to know, Jamie," he'd told her sadly.

Unfortunately, Jamie knew only too well how intractable her mother could be. To discover she had a granddaughter brought up by two lesbians wasn't going to help win her round. In her mind, she had lost two children, her son to a bomb and her daughter to what she regarded as a disgusting lifestyle. At least, she had told Jamie on more than one occasion, she could be proud of her son.

Van touched Jamie's arm. She always seemed to know when Jamie needed her comforting presence.

✝

Taylor had a few weeks at home before starting the next phase of her training. Laurel had been worried she would be going to one of the southern bases, Winchester or Aldershot, but was relieved to find out it was Catterick, under two hours drive away. Maddie didn't know how she was going to cope when Tay finished there and went on to join her unit in some far-off place. It seemed Tay was hoping for a posting to Alberta in Canada. She had expressed an interest in tanks, and the conditions there were ideal for duplicating the kind of terrain that troops on the ground faced in desert places.

Maddie found Taylor alone in the conservatory one morning when Laurel was with a student, with only the faint sounds of a Chopin waltz being played badly disturbing the peaceful scene. She sat down across from her daughter who looked relaxed, sprawled out on the two-seater, her long legs hanging over one end.

She looked up from her phone. "What's up, Mads?"

"You and Annie. Is it serious?" She and Laurel had been surprised when Tay insisted Annie be invited along to her Passing Out ceremony. And during this leave period, Annie had become a permanent feature, staying over most nights.

Taylor sat up. "Of course it is."

"Well, you know. It's not fair on her if you're away all the time."

"Yeah, it's kinda hard. But we're connected." She waved her phone.

"What about if you do go somewhere like Canada?"

"We'll work it out. Like you always told me, don't worry about things until they happen."

"It doesn't generally work that way with relationships. We're just concerned. You two are a bit young to be committing yourselves to each other. And you're going to be travelling the world while Annie's stuck here."

"She's applying to Leicester. She wants to study ancient history and archaeology. That's pretty cool. She'll get to go places as well."

Maddie sighed. She was still adjusting to this new, grown-up version of their daughter who seemed to know exactly what she wanted and how she was going to get it.

"Okay. Good. You two seem to have worked things out. But don't forget, just because you're now a rough, tough soldier, we're still here when you need us."

"Thanks, Mads"

Maddie got up to leave.

"Oh, and by the way, I've already had this convo with Mum."

"You little shit!" Maddie lunged at her.

Tay swatted her away easily and laughed. "That's more like it!"

†

There were times when Sasha wondered if any of her time with Phoebe had been real. The lovemaking sessions had felt real. Was Phoebe always playing a part? Her capacity for telling stories so well honed that deception came so easily to her?

Sasha found it hard to accept that their whole relationship had been based on lies. After Cynthia's revelations, fortified by a second shot of brandy, she had gone home prepared to confront Phoebe only to find that she'd already gone. Closets emptied, computer leads trailing from the wall, bookshelves cleared. Predictably, she now thought, all the jewelry Sasha had given her was gone too. The note she eventually found next to the kettle simply said, "Thanks, babe. It's been fun, sometimes." The removal of all traces of her existence were so complete, she had to have had help. No doubt all planned during her afternoon session at the hotel. Sasha's first thought had been to try the Radisson to see if she was there. But neither Phoebe Lemming nor Felicity Lemon had checked in. Or Felix LeMar.

What was real now was the fact she couldn't afford the house payments. Why had she let Phoebe persuade her to buy a larger house than the two of them needed in such an affluent area? Her only hope of gaining solvency was an upturn in the housing market and a quick sale. She could see herself living in a one-room bedsit. Visions of Jamie's bare room assailed her in her darkest moments.

She'd lost her deposit on the Christmas holiday. Even if she had gone on her own, she hadn't been able to picture herself sitting by the poolside bar pretending to be a journalist. Memories of Christmases spent with Jamie in various exotic locations would have been unbearable anyway.

Trying to contact Jamie hadn't worked either. Her phone calls were blocked again and whenever she called the University, she was told the head of technical services was in a meeting.

When she had tried Phoebe's publisher for gaining information on her whereabouts, they said they didn't give out author's details, but they would let Miss Lemon know she'd called. After a few weeks when there was no word from Phoebe, she had swallowed what was left of her pride and gone to see Philip Pearlman. He had been uncharacteristically gracious, as he poured tea from his ridiculous looking teapot.

"No, I haven't heard from her. Not since we rejected her manuscript."

"So, were you leading her on? Telling her it was the new *Game of Thrones*?"

"I was just hoping to give her a push in the right direction. The story had potential, but she doesn't really have what it takes to write a good fantasy or sci-fi novel."

Sasha was thankful her instincts on that front hadn't failed her. All her others had though. She had been thoroughly deceived.

The only glimmer of brightness in her existence had come when she saw a review for the new Felicity Lemon book in The Guardian. The reviewer couldn't resist punning that the latest Lemon was a lemon. Not worth a read even if offered free on Kindle Unlimited. So whatever boost to her writing career Phoebe had perhaps hoped for with her new lover, it had tanked spectacularly.

She sat in the mostly empty house, having sold all the expensive items of furniture apart from the bed and the sofa, the one she had given Jamie. If she breathed deeply she would catch a whiff of Stevie's scent. Her eyes were drawn to the picture on the wall. The one possession of value she couldn't bear to part with. A tear trickled out as she sought out the shadowy image of the black cat in the window.

†

Sitting out in the sun with her father, Jamie felt relaxed for the first time in two days. There had been the emotional reunion with her dad, introducing him to Van, to Taylor's parents, and then Taylor herself. Attending the Passing Out ceremony had brought out mixed feelings of pride and distress. Just being in military surroundings for that short time had been hard for both of them.

Now, though, they were sitting outside on the newly finished patio enjoying a glass of wine. Stevie was lying in a patch of sunlight by her feet. When Van went back into the house to bring out the food for their *al fresco* lunch, her father spoke quietly.

"I like her much better than the last one."

"Really. I had no idea you didn't like Sasha."

"She wasn't right for you."

It took all her self-control not to break down in front of him.

"So, when are you going to ask Ivana to marry you? You can do that now, can't you?"

Jamie blinked back her tears. "I'm not ready for that yet."

"When will you be ready? You're over fifty now, sweetheart. Life's too short, as we both know. When you find happiness, grab it with both hands. That's my motto these days."

Jamie looked down the garden at the trees, now in full leaf. "Do you think she would say yes, if I asked her?"

"I'm certain of it. She makes you happy in a way I've not seen before. And the way she looks at you, I've no doubt she's in love."

The cat at her feet stirred and stretched. He jumped up onto her lap and made himself comfortable. Jamie stroked his black fur, warmed by the sun, and thought of all the changes that had taken place in the past eight or nine months. It was true she was happier than she'd ever thought she could be again. The struggles of the previous autumn were now a fading memory. The worry over the abnormal smear test, the shock of seeing Sasha again, rescuing her girlfriend, and almost losing her own. Finding out she had a niece, promoted at work into a job she was now enjoying, these had been the positive points. But the highlight of it all was finding it was possible to love again. She looked back towards the house and saw Van watching her from the kitchen window.

†

Van would move in with Jamie if she asked. She was spending all her weekends with her as it was and sometimes a night or two during the week. Renting out her flat would give her some funds while she looked for another job. It was time she moved on and found something more fulfilling.

But she understood Jamie's reticence about offering a permanent living arrangement. Having been hurt so badly by the breakup with Sasha, she wasn't likely to risk it again anytime soon.

They had spent Christmas together, which included a Christmas and Boxing Day visit with her parents. Jamie had charmed them both, and patiently helped her mother with a thousand-piece jigsaw while Van and her dad watched the football.

Stevie had been left with Taylor who, much to Jamie's surprise, managed to persuade Laurel to let him stay with them. Van suspected, though, it was more in an effort on her friend's part to keep her family together for the festivities than any sudden affection for the cat. Taylor would have happily done the cat-sitting in Jamie's house but her mother wasn't going to allow that to happen.

She still experienced pangs of jealousy. The week before Christmas two cards had arrived for Jamie. One for her birthday on the twenty-second, and one for Christmas. Both from Sasha. And signed only by her. The distress must have been evident on her face so Jamie showed her the envelopes. They'd been forwarded from her former address.

"That's the only address she has for me, Van. I haven't given her this one."

"Does she still phone you?"

"No."

Now, six months down the line, she was watching Jamie, sitting in the garden with her father. Robert Steele was a good-looking man, tanned from the years spent living in a sunnier climate. She could see where Jamie got her looks and mannerisms. They were very much alike. Van wondered about the mother, how she could have cut them both off so completely. There had been no cards from her at Christmas. Jamie hadn't wanted anyone to make a fuss over her fiftieth birthday, but you would have thought her mother would at least have sent a card.

Jamie looked up and caught her staring. She smiled, the killer smile, the one that never failed to melt her insides.

Van smiled back. No good fretting over what might or might not happen. She had waited this long to find the love of her life, she could wait a bit longer for an invitation to take her place by her side.

About the Author

Jen Silver

Jen lives near Hebden Bridge in West Yorkshire with her long-term partner whom she married in December 2014. She has always enjoyed reading an eclectic range of genres including sci-fi, fantasy, historical fiction and lesbian fiction. As well as reading and writing, other activities include golf and archery. Her firsthand experience of an archaeological dig and a lifelong interest in Roman history were the creative forces behind her first published novel, *Starting Over,* released by Affinity in October 2014. The second book in the series, *Arc Over Time*, was published in May 2015 and the third book, *Carved in Stone*, in February 2016. Jen insists that she didn't set out to write a trilogy, but the characters demanded a proper conclusion to the story. *The Circle Dance*, published in March 2016, is a standalone story.

Contact Jen at jenjsilver@yahoo.co.uk, friend her on Facebook, or visit her blog: https://jenjsilver.wordpress.com

Other Books from Affinity eBook Press

Take Me As I Am by JM Dragon & Erin O'Reilly When Jo Lackerly and Thea Danvers meet, an unexpected friendship develops, proving a catalyst for both women to change their lives irrevocably. Follow them on a journey of discovery that will have your heart smiling, blood boiling, and senses entangled in a wonderful romance.

Carved in Stone by Jen Silver Join the characters from Starting Over and Arc Over Time in this final book from the Starling Hill trilogy. Ellie Winters thinks she might be going mad when the ancient queen wants a proper burial for herself and her consort. *Carved in Stone* has romance, adventure, a treasure hunt, and a happy endings for all, living and dead.

Anywhere, Everywhere by Renee MacKenzie Gwen Martin's life in the Ten Thousand Islands area changes irrevocably when Piper Jackson comes into her life. Without trust, can the budding relationship between Gwen and Piper survive? Or will the answers to the questions continue to haunt them?

Venus Rising by Ali Spooner Levi Johnson arrives at Venus Rising, an exclusive lesbian only tropical resort in the Virgin Islands and finds more than she expected—a sizzling hot love triangle. Torn between her attraction to both women struggles to choose the right woman to share her life.

The Devil's Tree by Ali Spooner Torn between her love for the pack and her need to find what's missing in her life Devin Benoit travels to New Orleans. Will the previous happenings at the Devil's Tree help or hinder Devin in the fight of her life, and the life of Tia, the woman who now owns her heart?

The Beggars' Coppice by Erica Lawson Edda Case is a woman in crisis who discovers that things are not as they seem. Is it truly a message for her from beyond the grave or is something more sinister taking place? Can Edda solve the mystery of *The Beggars' Coppice*?

Locked Inside by Annette Mori How much does the power of love matter to someone who must overcome obstacles far greater than most people face in a lifetime.

Line of Sight by Ali Spooner Sasha and her lover Kara are back. Continue the thrilling adventures of this couple from the Sasha Thibodaux series.

Requiem for Vukovar by Angela Koenig Requiem for Vukovar continues the Refraction series and the exploits of Jeri O'Donnell and her partner, Kelly Corcoran. In an epic siege largely ignored by the wider world, Kelly, who was prepared to give up comforts and certainties when she became part of Jeri's nomadic life, encounters more than physical danger. Her ability to maintain her core integrity is assaulted by the inevitable ugliness of war. For Jeri, the true battle is confronting her attraction to violence as she struggles against losing herself in the exhilaration of combat.

Against All Odds by JM Dragon From award winning and bestselling author JM Dragon, with significant updates by, Erin O'Reilly comes an original tale of romance where everything seems to be stacked against two women whose destinies bring them together. Life however takes a twisted path setting both Steph and Louise in directions they never thought possible. Will love win out against all odds or will love be forever lost?

The Settlement by Ali Spooner The outpouring of love and friendship toward Cadin helps her on her path to healing and learning to trust her heart to love once again. Join bestselling author Ali Spooner on this sensational journey that ends with a heartwarming romance.

Once Upon a Time by Alane Hotchkin Raven only wanted to escape the blows that life had dealt her. She longed to be on the open sea and free. When she came upon a beautiful young girl sitting alone in the middle of a meadow, little did she know that her destiny would be changed forever. Will they become the pawns of the ancient vision or will both paths lead to the same port of destiny? Find out it in this exciting high seas adventure that will capture your imagination.

Asset Management by Annette Mori Follow the twists and turns to the explosive conclusion. Not everything is black and white. There are many shades of gray and sometimes it's difficult to decipher who is good and who is evil. No one is all virtue or all malevolence, but sometimes love helps us rise above.

Do Dreams Come True? by JM Dragon How do two people who really shouldn't get on end up in a relationship? Find out in this deliciously ordinary romance.

Return to Me by Erin O'Reilly Will Salvation bring just that to Ellie, allowing her to find peace and happiness again, or will it have her questioning all that she believes in? A wonderful romance cloaked within an intriguing mystery.

Arc Over Time by Jen Silver This wonderful romantic continuation with the characters from *Starting Over* ties up loose ends. But the question is—does everyone have a happy ending? A must read.

The Presence by Charlene Neal Can Rebecca and Kayleigh overcome ghosts from the past and their own insecurities, or will a presence from the past tear them apart?

A Walk Away by Lacey Schmidt Sometimes chance brings you to the right person to help you resolve some of your baggage, and you learn to like yourself a little more. Kat and Rand are smart enough to recognize this chance in each other, but they also find that there is a catch to every opportunity—walking toward something is always walking away from something else.

Possessing Morgan by Erica Lawson The investigation has barely begun when Andrea becomes the target of a nearly fatal hit-and-run. But was it really aimed at her? Can she and Morgan find the common ground they need to solve the case and stop the attacks, or are the gaps just too wide to bridge?

Twenty-three Miles by Renee MacKenzie This is a story about community, and how it comes together in dangerous and devastating times. When you don't know who to trust, you better have friends who will rally around you. Will Talia and Shay find the answers they need to the mystery of the murders on the parkway, or will justice be elusive? Will they survive their quest for the truth?

Reece's Star by TJ Vertigo Under Faith's guiding, loving hand, will Reece successfully traverse the rocky road of emotion and embrace the positive changes in her life? Or will she panic and be unable to control that Animal part of herself? Will she take that next step to declare herself fully capable of love and devotion? This third installment in the popular series that began with *Private Dancer* continues the passionate and often hilarious romance of Reece and Faith as they both grow in love and in trust.

Confined Spaces by Renee MacKenzie Corporate politics, complicated romance, and long distances conspire to keep

Andie and Kara all boxed in. Can love triumph despite the Confined Spaces?

Cowgirl Up by Ali Spooner Ride along with the MC2, for boot scootin', butt kickin', dirt eatin', rodeo adventures, with a love story thrown into the mix.

If I Were a Boy by Erin O'Reilly Will Katie and Helen be able to make a life together work or succumb to doubts and the pressures of family? This story will fill you with the thrill of passion and the tenderness of love.

The Chronicles of Ratha: Book 2 A Lion Among the Lambs by Erica Lawson Can Jordana believe in herself like her Noorthi sisters do? Only then can she fulfill her destiny as The Chosen One. Follow the colorful cast of characters in this action-packed adventure sequel as they traverse the galaxy. Of course, nothing ever goes smoothly when Jordana is involved.

Terminal Event by Ali Spooner Will the killer be caught or continue to evade authorities? Can Tally and Blair's budding romance survive the possibility? Read this intense murder mystery romance and find out.

Love Forever, Live Forever by Annette Mori Fate intervenes and puts Nicky directly back into the path of her first love, Sara, and the corresponding events send her into a tailspin. Now she must decide—who will be the person she ends up living with and loving forever?

The One by JM Dragon *2015 GCLS Winner for Romance, Intrigue, and Adventure. The One* is a romance with everything, love, intrigue, misunderstandings with a happy conclusion—the only question—who gets the girl?

Reflected Passion by Erica Lawson Through a mirror, Françoise embraces life anew, while for Dale it is a powerful awakening, forcing her to discover not only her sensual nature, but the inner strength she possesses.

Flight by Renee Mackenzie Some lives will be lost and others changed forever when the sisters' lives intersect. Will they be consumed by the wreckage, or will they be able to pick themselves up and take flight?

Starting Over by Jen Silver Book 1 of the Starling Hill Trilogy. There's a mystery afoot—whose royal resting place is disturbed at Starling Hill? All is revealed in this classic romance of simmering passions, anguished loss, and the wonder of love.

The One by JM Dragon Rosa Moran is a woman with a mission. Philomena Casters is the pilot sent to bring Rosa a letter that encourages her to return to England when a family member falls ill. This is a romance with everything—love, intrigue, misunderstandings, and two women whose faith and trust allow them to overcome all obstacles thrown at them.

E-Books, Print, Free e-books

Visit our website for more publications available online.

www.affinityebooks.com

Published by Affinity E-Book Press NZ LTD
Canterbury, New Zealand

Registered Company 2517228

www.ingramcontent.com/pod-product-compliance
Lightning Source LLC
Chambersburg PA
CBHW060549260626
47161CB00003B/1119